"*Are* you trying to take advantage of me?" Mona asked

The question sounded incredibly innocent. The waves of desire that her undeniable nearness was fanning definitely weren't.

Every fiber of his being wanted to give in, but he continued to fight it. "No, I'm—"

The rest of his adamant protest went unspoken. He found it impossible to speak when Mona's lips were suddenly and firmly pressed against his.

She was quick—he'd give her that.

He tasted her moan and felt the blood surge through his veins as if it had been set on fire. Maybe it had been.

He needed to put a stop to this. In a moment. Just one more moment.

He promised himself that he would do the right thing in a moment, but right now, just for this erotic half a heartbeat, he wanted to enjoy this completely unexpected turn of events.

Dear Reader,

Here we are, back again in Forever, Texas. This time we're going to explore two people who have loved each other but put up a lot of resistance along the way. Luckily, love does prevail. The neatest part of writing is that I know there will be a happy ending, no matter how rocky the path is for my characters. If life were perfect, my husband, son and daughter would read from the dialogue pages I have given them and act accordingly. But life isn't perfect, and I have very independent people in my world who make life one surprise after another. Which works, too, and, I have to admit, keeps me on my toes. It also helps me write, because ideas come from all over and my family has appeared over and over again in all my books. You might stumble across my husband here. I'm not saying any more.

As ever, I thank you for reading, and from the bottom of my heart I wish you someone to love who loves you back.

Best,

Marie Ferrarella

Ramona and the Renegade

MARIE FERRARELLA

HARLEQUIN®

TORONTO • NEW YORK • LONDON
AMSTERDAM • PARIS • SYDNEY • HAMBURG
STOCKHOLM • ATHENS • TOKYO • MILAN • MADRID
PRAGUE • WARSAW • BUDAPEST • AUCKLAND

Recycling programs
for this product may
not exist in your area.

ISBN-13: 978-0-373-75342-0

RAMONA AND THE RENEGADE

Copyright © 2011 by Marie Rydzynski-Ferrarella

ABOUT THE AUTHOR

Marie Ferrarella is a *USA TODAY* bestselling and RITA®
Award-winning author who has written more than two
hundred books for Silhouette and Harlequin Books,
some under the name of Marie Nicole. Her romances
are beloved by fans worldwide. Visit her website at
www.marieferrarella.com.

Books by Marie Ferrarella

To
Nicholas
The sky is the limit.
You just have to believe.
I do.

Chapter One ·

He recognized the car immediately.

On his way home, hoping to beat the predicted flash floods, Deputy Sheriff Joe Lone Wolf brought his four-wheel-drive vehicle to a halt the moment he spotted the other car.

The rain was falling faster and harder with each quarter hour that went by. Because of that, his range of visibility was considerably shortened. It hampered him somewhat, but Joe still would have known the battered Jeep anywhere.

It was ten years old, silver, with a red door on its passenger side thanks to an unexpected, sudden meeting with a hundred-foot bitternut hickory tree one foggy night. With some effort on his part, Mick Henley, Forever, Texas's best—and only—mechanic, had managed to find an exact match to replace the Jeep's mangled door.

Well, almost exact. It would have needed two coats of silver paint to make it the same color as the rest of the vehicle. But Ramona Santiago had fallen in love with the bold red color and refused to change it once the new door was in place.

Red suited her.

It matched her personality, Joe had thought at the time.

He still did.

Mona was all things wild and bold. Far from shy and retiring, the raven-haired, green-eyed beauty had all the subdued qualities of a Fourth of July firecracker in the middle of exploding. The green eyes came from her Irish ancestors, the midnight-black hair was a gift from the rest of her heritage—Mexican and Apache.

They had the last in common.

Deputy Joe Lone Wolf was an Apache, through and through, born on the nearby Apache reservation where he spent his younger years before his uncle finally up-rooted him and transplanted him into Forever proper, thereby rescuing him from an early demise.

He and Mona had something else in common—she was the sheriff's younger sister, and he was technically in Rick Santiago's employ. One of three deputies, Joe had been with Rick and on the job the longest, although only by a matter of a few months.

If Rick knew that his sister was coming back to Forever tonight, he hadn't mentioned anything. Joe had a strong suspicion that the sheriff would be just as surprised as he was that Mona was here. The last anyone had heard, Mona was due to reach Forever the day before her brother's wedding.

Why the change in schedule? Joe wondered.

The vehicle's windshield wipers were already set on maximum speed and were clearly losing the battle for visibility against the rain. He would have had better luck seeing if he just stuck his head out the side window.

But he'd seen enough, approaching on the gently inclining slope, to know that something was definitely wrong. Mona's Jeep was stationary in a place where no one would willingly choose to stop. Moreover, Mona wasn't in the vehicle but was standing outside it.

Specifically, Mona was in the process of wrestling with a tire iron, cursing the very flat front passenger tire that was, of necessity, the focus of all her attention.

Though never demure, the Mona he recalled didn't ordinarily turn the air blue around her. She'd obviously been at this for a bit and, just as obviously, been unsuccessful in her endeavor to change the tire.

Just the slightest hint of amusement ran through him, even though it made no appearance on his face. He knew better than that. Mona had eyes in the back of her pretty head. At least, she did before she'd gone off to college to become a veterinarian.

Parking his vehicle several feet away from hers, Joe got out and, braving the rain, approached the sheriff's sister from behind. She didn't appear to hear him, but under the circumstances, that was more than understandable. The wind howled, the rain pelted and made its own mournful noise, and Mona, damsel-in-distress in this scenario, was cursing.

Loudly.

With all this going on, Joe doubted if she could have heard a train approaching from a distance.

"Don't you know you have to sweet-talk a car to get it to cooperate?" Joe asked just as he came to where Mona was standing.

The next thing he knew, he was literally jumping back, out of her reach, and not a moment too soon.

Startled, Mona immediately turned the tire iron in her hands into a weapon and swung it at her invisible target for all she was worth.

"Hey!" Joe cried indignantly, barely avoiding being separated from his midsection by the metal tool.

Tired, annoyed at the sudden downpour that had wreaked havoc with her schedule, and furious with the tire that had almost caused her to go careening off the road and down into a ditch, Mona was definitely not at her best. In addition to that, the knowledge that, at this moment, she bore a strong resemblance to a resuscitated drowned rat did nothing to improve her mood.

When she saw who it was, she let go of the tire iron, dropping it to the ground. After a beat. She took in a deep, shaky breath, trying not to think about what might have happened if Joe's reflexes hadn't been as good as they were.

"Joe, you scared me!" she snapped. Turning the bolt of fear that shot through her into anger and aiming it at Joe.

"Then I guess we're even." His voice was calm, but beneath the deadly still exterior he had to admit he was anything but. Moving in closer again, Joe looked down at the tire that was still very much a part of Mona's vehicle. She hadn't gotten very far in her attempt to remove it, he noted. Raising his eyes to hers, he asked, "Got a flat?"

Mona laughed shortly and shook her head. "I always did love the way you could grasp any situation at lightning speed."

His expression never changed. "It was a rhetorical comment."

She pushed her plastered wet hair out of her eyes with the back of her hand. "So was mine."

With the rain beating a faster and faster tattoo on his tan, worn Stetson as it showered down all around him, Joe gave her a long, measuring look.

For the most part, Mona had been away at college, then veterinarian school these past eight years. Although it didn't seem possible, every time she came back, she seemed even more beautiful than when she'd left. But her sharp tongue hadn't dulled a whit. He supposed that there were just some things in life you could count on.

"You want some help or not?" Joe asked, quietly eyeing her.

Mona had made it a point never to ask for help. It was a matter of pride with her. Plus, if she wasn't counting on anyone, if she didn't depend on anyone, then she would never have to go through the agony of disappointment again. It was a philosophy she was forced to develop very early in life, when she finally realized that her mother would never come back for them the way she'd promised.

The only exceptions to Mona's philosophy were her brother, her late grandmother and Doc Whitmore. Over the years, the latter had slowly became the father she'd never known, as well as her mentor. Those were the three who'd brought stability into her life.

As for Joe, well, Joe was someone she'd gone to school with. Someone who'd always managed to be somewhere in close proximity, like the air and the trees. One way or another, Joe seemed never to be that far out of range. In short, he'd been her best friend, though neither one of them had ever verbally acknowledged the role.

She might have known she'd run into him before she saw anyone else from Forever, Mona thought.

In response to his offer for help, her slender shoulders rose and fell in a careless shrug beneath her soaked jacket. "Well, since you're here and all..."

As she spoke, she stepped back from the defunct vehicle. Because of the torrential rain and the dust now swiftly turning into mud, Mona found her footing compromised. She was about to slip backward and come perilously close to ignobly landing on her butt if not her back altogether. At the last second, she was rescued from the impending embarrassment by Joe's quick reflexes. He grabbed her, pulling her forward toward him before she could slide backward. Due to his strength, the abrupt motion was a matter of overcompensation and suddenly, rather than discovering herself sprawled out on the ground and flat against the oozing mud, Mona slammed up against Joe without so much as the width of a raindrop between them.

She raised her eyes to Joe's, doing her best to regroup as quickly as possible. Her pulse raced and she didn't like it. She also didn't want him taking any note of it.

"Is that your heart pounding?" she asked flippantly, doing her very best to sound as nonchalant as she didn't feel.

"Nope," he lied. "Must be yours."

The same strong hands that had grabbed her now pushed her back by a good twelve inches, if not more. Having Mona against him like that took control out of his hands.

"You're an accident waiting to happen," he told her, his voice flat, emotionless as he tried to deflect any more attention away from the state of the organ that was betraying him.

Or *one* of the organs that were betraying him at any rate, he thought ruefully.

He nodded toward his vehicle that was parked off to the side. "Why don't you just go and wait in my car while I handle this?"

She was *not* about to take a chance on slipping again so soon. The last thing she wanted was to hear him laughing at her.

"What? And miss the learning experience of a life-time, watching you change a tire?" she scoffed, raising her voice so that the winds didn't whip it away. "How will poor little me ever learn how to do such a big, manly thing if I'm shut away in an ivory tower?"

For emphasis, she waved toward the vehicle which became less visible despite its close proximity.

Joe shook his head. "I see you still have a smart mouth."

The grin on her lips was deliberately exaggerated. She batted her eyelashes at him like an old-fashioned movie goddess. "It goes with my smart mind."

"Then I guess you must be brilliant by now," he commented drily.

Moving slowly, he picked his way around her Jeep, going to the rear.

"I am," Mona answered in the same tone, punctuating her sentence with a toss of her wet head. "Where are you going?"

He glanced in her direction. "Someone with your

brilliant mind would know that I wanted to check the condition of your spare before going through the trouble of taking off the flat."

"I knew that," she retorted, then added in a more mellow tone, "but I didn't know if you did." She followed him to the rear of her vehicle.

The spare tire was mounted on the back of the Jeep. Testing the tire's integrity, Joe frowned and shook his head. This was not good. He spared her a glance over his shoulder and could see by her body language that she'd become instantly defensive before he even said a word. He said it anyway.

"Don't you ever check the condition of your spare?"

Her eyes narrowed beneath her soggy bangs. "Somewhere between studying for my finals—and the examination for my vet license—and juggling a part-time job to pay for little incidentals like food, it must have temporarily fallen off my 'immediately to do' list."

He ignored her sarcastic tone and answered matter-of-factly. "Well, that's a shame," he told her. "Because your spare's flat, too."

Mona closed her eyes. It figured. All things considered, this had not been one of her better days. Opening her eyes again, she looked at Joe. "As flat as the one on it?" she asked.

You just didn't substitute one flat tire for another. Flat was flat. His dark eyes would have pinned her to the wall—if there had been one around. "You know better than that."

Yes, she did. She was just desperate. And really, really annoyed. With both tires for being flat and with herself for not noticing that the spare had slowly lost its air. And most of all, right now she was annoyed with Joe for pointing it out.

Hands fisted at her waist, Mona swung one booted foot at the right front tire and kicked it.

"That's not going to make it come back to life," Joe commented.

She glared at him. "I know that." The hood she had on provided next to no protection for her at this point and when it slid off her head, she didn't bother to try to pull it back up. "Now what?"

The weather seemed to be getting more hostile by the moment. He turned so that the rain was at his back. Because he was taller, he provided a little shelter for her, as well.

He gave her options, although only one was really viable. "Well, I could call Mick and you could wait here for him to come with his tow truck—if you don't wash away first. Or I could give you a ride into town and you could talk to Mick yourself, face-to-face."

Mona was in no mood to share a car ride with him, even though she knew it was her best bet. "No third option, huh?"

"Sure." Joe raised his voice again, competing with the increasing sound of the wind and the rain. "You could wait here for the tire spirits to come and perform the miracle of the reinflating tire."

His expression was so serious that anyone not knowing Joe would have thought that he actually believed in the spirits he'd just invoked. But she had grown up witnessing displays of his deadpan sense of humor.

With a sigh, Mona resigned herself to her only real

alternative. "I guess I'll have to pick option number two."

"Good choice," he answered.

Turning on his heel, he started to lead the short distance back to his parked vehicle. It took him less than a minute to realize that Mona wasn't following behind him. He stopped and looked over his shoulder. She was still next to her Jeep.

"Change your mind?"

Crawling into the rear of the vehicle, Mona hauled out a large suitcase. She had no choice but to set it down in the mud.

"No," she told him, "I don't want anyone making off with my clothes." She didn't bother looking at him as she leaned into the back and grabbed a second suitcase. This one, lodged behind the driver's seat, proved to be less cooperative and she struggled to get it out of the vehicle.

Joe shook his head at the woman's unadulterated stubbornness. He crossed back to her in a couple of long strides. Firmly taking hold of her shoulders for a second time, he moved her out of the way and easily pulled the large suitcase out. Instead of putting it down next to the first one, he held on to it, keeping it out of the mud.

Mona squared her shoulders. "I could have managed," she protested.

Arguing with her served no purpose. "No one said you couldn't," he answered. Still holding one suitcase, he deliberately picked up the other with his free hand. "This it?" he asked. "Or are there more?"

She'd never been one to be careless with her hard-earned money, but she had accumulated a few things in the past eight years. "The rest are being shipped," she told him.

Something small and hopeful zipped through him. He banked it down quickly, giving absolutely no indication of its momentary existence. Instead, he asked in what passed for a disinterested voice, "You moving back?"

She wanted to. But there were things she needed to work out. Not to mention that her brother had said he had other plans for her, plans that included having her move to a large city. She didn't want to disappoint him, but Forever was really the only home she ever knew. The only place she'd ever felt she really belonged.

"For now," she allowed.

Joe weighed her tone and made a judgment.

He was forced to raise his voice yet again as he walked to his vehicle. The wind grew louder, the rain more harsh. He felt as if his words were being snatched away even as he uttered them.

"Set your sights on somewhere else?" he asked.

She had nothing to carry but the shoulder bag that had seen her through both college and veterinarian school. Holding it tightly against her, Mona moved quickly to keep up. At this point, she wanted nothing more than to get out of the rain and curl up somewhere warm and dry. In lieu of that, Joe's car would do.

"Not me," she told Joe, then repeated the words when he looked at her quizzically. Satisfied he'd heard her, she added, "Rick."

Reaching his vehicle, Joe loaded first one suitcase, then the other into the backseat. When he turned to look at Mona, she had already scrambled into the passenger seat in the front.

He opened the driver's-side door and got in. "You want to explain that?"

Mona felt around for the seat belt. Finding it, she secured it around herself. "Rick—" She realized she was still yelling and lowered her voice. "Rick has high hopes that I'll move to the big city, open an animal hospital and be a big success."

"And you?" He put his key into the ignition, but didn't turn it just yet. "What are your hopes?"

Mona ran her hands up and down her arms, trying not to shiver. It was unseasonably cold for spring.

"To get dry again," she answered.

She glanced out the side window. The rain was getting worse, but that wasn't what was bothering her. She heard a distant muffled roar and it was getting louder. That could only mean one thing. She turned toward Joe. Now wasn't the time for any false bravado or stubborn ploys on her part. They had trouble.

"Joe—"

Joe turned the key and after a what seemed like an unnaturally long moment, the engine caught and turned over.

"Yeah, I know," he answered. "Looks like we're in for it."

They both knew what he was talking about. "It" was Joe's loose reference to the flash floods that they were periodically subjected to when Mother Nature decided to be too bountiful with her supply of rain and drenched the lands far too quickly to be of any actual benefit to anyone.

Mona twisted around in her seat, looking back at her vehicle. She knew she had no choice, but she really hated leaving it behind.

"My car," she protested.

"We'll find it once it stops raining," Joe told her with an assurance that defied argument.

She turned back around and sat facing forward again. Mona watched as his car's windshield wipers vainly battled the downpour, losing ground with every stroke they spasmodically made. To her dismay, the man beside her slowed down and began driving at a speed that would have brought shame to an arthritic turtle.

The fearless daredevil she'd once known would have laughed at the rain and gone full throttle into the storm. But that boy was gone now and in his place was a cautious man who thought things through.

She knew that any faster and they risked driving off the road and landing in a ditch.

Or worse.

Another thought suddenly struck her. She turned to look at his profile. "We're not going to make it into town, are we?"

If this had been anyone else in the car with him, he might have uttered some platitude meant to be reassuring, doling out a spoonful of hope to someone he knew was silently asking for it.

But this wasn't anyone else. This was Mona. Mona, who took every white lie as an affront, every sugar-coated fib as an insult to her intelligence. So he said the only thing he knew she would tolerate.

He told her the truth.

"Nope."

Chapter Two

"'Nope'?"

Stunned, Mona repeated the single-syllable answer Joe had just uttered. If they couldn't reach town, that meant the oncoming flash flood would cut off access to Forever.

But she knew Joe, knew him as well as she knew herself and her brother. Joe was not the type to merely give up or surrender, even if his adversary was Nature itself.

Still, the seconds ticked by and he wasn't saying anything beyond the one word he'd already uttered. Mona felt herself growing antsy, in direct correlation to the force of the storm.

If they couldn't make it to town, they would have to find shelter somewhere. They couldn't stay out in the open. Flash floods were known to sweep vehicles away in the blink of an eye.

"Say something, already," she ordered, then immediately added a warning. "I swear, Joe Lone Wolf, if I hear you say, 'Today is a good day to die,' you are going to really, really regret it."

He stole a quick glance in her direction, taking care

not to look away from the road for more than half a heartbeat. Visibility was next to impossible, but at this point, he was searching for something very specific.

"So much for my one dramatic moment," he quipped. "How about, 'Let's hole up in the old Murphy place until this passes'? Will that get me beat up, too?" he asked.

"The Murphy place?" Mona repeated uncertainly. She hadn't realized that she'd gotten this disoriented. She squinted as she peered through the all but obliterated windshield. Visibility was down to approximately twelve to eighteen inches in front of the vehicle, maybe less. "Is that around here?"

The "Murphy place" was little more than a three-room cabin that by urban standards hardly qualified as a vacation getaway, much less a regular home. It was more in the realm of a shack, really. More than three quarters of a century old, it had once been the center of a dream—and a budding cattle ranch—until an outbreak of anthrax had eventually killed both. The cabin, which should have been the beginning of a sprawling ranch house, had stood empty for close to twenty years now, after the last descendent of Jonas Murphy died without leaving any heirs, just a mountain of bad debts.

Somehow in all that time, the building, a veritable feasting ground for vermin, had managed to escape being torn down or even claimed. No one cared enough about the unproductive piece of land to buy it and begin building something from scratch again. So the decaying cabin stood, enduring the seasons year after year and, like an aging octogenarian with osteoporosis, it grew steadily more and more frail.

The last time he'd passed this way and actually looked at the cabin, Joe had thought that the only thing keeping the building up were probably the termites, holding hands.

He sincerely hoped that they were holding tight for at least one more night.

Instincts that were generations in the making guided him toward where he had last seen the cabin this morning on his way into town.

"It should be close by," he answered Mona, then spared her a grin and added, "Unless those pesky tire spirits decided to move it just so that they could annoy you some more."

She doubted that it was possible to annoy her any more than she already was, Mona thought. "Very funny."

The grin on Joe's face softened into a smile and then that faded, as well. He found that he had to fight not just the rain but the wind for control over his vehicle. He sensed Mona's tension. She was watching him.

"Nothing to be afraid of," he assured her quietly as he continued to stare intently through the blinding rain.

Mona bristled. "I'm not afraid," she retorted, stopping just short of snapping at him.

She hated the fact that Joe could read her so well, that all he had to do was just look at her to sense what she was thinking. What bothered her most of all was that she couldn't return the "compliment" and do the same with him. It just didn't seem fair.

"Okay," Joe allowed. "Then why are you about to rip off my dashboard?" he asked. Without looking, he nodded in the general direction of her hands which were gripping the aforementioned dashboard.

Mona gritted her teeth. *Damn it.*

She was completely unaware that she was gripping the dashboard. Swallowing a curse, Mona dropped her hands into her lap, trying hard not to clench them.

"Just bracing myself for the inevitable crash. You're not exactly the best driver in the world," she reminded him pointedly.

He knew what she was referring to. At thirteen, he'd been angry at the world in general and specifically at the absentee father he'd never known and his mother, who'd died suddenly three years earlier. He'd been passed around from relative to relative and raised by committee, which compelled him to steal one of the elders' cars just to thumb his nose at everyone.

For the space of half an hour, he'd felt like his own man, free and independent. But the joyride ended when he lost control of the car and ended up in a ditch.

Miraculously emerging unscathed, he'd wound up working the entire summer and half the fall to pay off the repair bill for the car. He figured the episode would always haunt him, no matter what he might go on to accomplish in life. He didn't mind. He considered himself lucky to have walked away alive, much less without so much as a scratch.

What amused him about the whole thing is that Mona had a similar incident in her past. It had happened when she was ten. Rather than a joyride, after an argument with her grandmother Mona decided to run away from home. She took her grandmother's car to enable her escape. But the adventure was short-lived. Mona managed to go down only two streets before her grandmother had caught up to her—on foot. Even at that age, the old woman had been swift.

The car sustained no damage. The same, he knew, couldn't be said for Mona's posterior or her dignity. She was grounded for a month.

"I wouldn't throw rocks if I were you," he said, leaving it at that. When she frowned, he knew that she knew exactly what he was referring to.

A second later, Mona sat up straight in her seat, suddenly animated. "I see it. You were right. The cabin *is* here."

"Nice to know you have faith in me," Joe cracked, tightening his grip on the steering wheel. It was getting harder to keep the vehicle from veering.

"It's raining horses and steers," Mona cried, gesturing at the windshield and doing one better than what she considered to be the stereotypical comment about cats and dogs. "Anyone could have gotten turned around in this storm."

"*Most* people could have gotten turned around," he allowed. Things like that never happened to him. He took his natural sense of direction for granted.

She sighed, shaking her head. Same old Joe, she thought. "Despite what you think, you are not mystically empowered, Joe Lone Wolf."

Not for one minute did he think of himself as having any special, otherworldly powers, but he couldn't resist teasing her. "I came to your rescue out of the blue, didn't I?"

"You were just on your way home and stumbled across me," she corrected. "You've been taking the same route ever since you went to work for my brother as one of his deputies."

He turned the tables on her with ease. "Are you saying you took this path on purpose?" he asked, feigning surprise. "Just to run into me?"

"No, I'm saying that you—I mean, that I—" This wasn't coming out right. He was getting her all tongue-tied. Mona gave up. "Oh, hell, think what you want—but you *do* know better than that."

Yeah, he thought, he did. Had known it from the first moment that he'd laid eyes on Ramona as she walked into his second-period tenth-grade English class that February morning ten years ago. She'd been so beautiful to look at that it hurt him right down to his very core.

And right from the beginning he knew that girls like Ramona Santiago did not wind up with guys like him. He was an Apache through and through and it wasn't all that long ago that people regarded Native Americans like him as beneath them.

Granted, Mona, like her brother, was one third Apache herself, but it was the other two thirds of her, the Mexican-American and especially the Irish side of her, that carried all the weight. And those two thirds would have never welcomed a poor Apache teenager into her life in any other capacity than just as a friend.

So a friend he was. Someone for her to talk to, confide in if the spirit so moved her. Being her friend—her sometimes confidant—he'd long since decided is what made his life worth living. And what had, ultimately, made him abandon the wild, bad boy who didn't play by the rules and take up the straight-and-narrow path instead. The guy he had been would never have pinned on a badge and sworn an oath to it. But he'd done it for her, for Ramona.

She probably hadn't had a clue, he thought now.

Just as she didn't have a clue about the rest of it. About his feelings for her. And he intended for it to stay that way.

Resisting the urge to speed up just a little, Joe slowly drove the Jeep up to the rickety cabin that had once been home to an entire family.

Silently breathing a sigh of relief, he pulled up the hand brake as he turned off the engine.

Mona, he noticed, hadn't undone her seat belt. "Something wrong?" he asked her.

"Is it safe?" she asked, eyeing the cabin uncertainly. There'd been ghost stories about the cabin when she'd been growing up. She didn't believe those for a minute, but the cabin did look as if it was about to blow away in the next big gust of wind.

Joe knew that the cabin wasn't as structurally sound as some of the newer buildings in town, but he really didn't expect it to fall down around them—unless one of the termites sneezed, he thought, suppressing a smile.

"It's standing and it's dry inside," he pointed out. "Or reasonably so," he added, figuring that time had been hard on the roof and there had to be places where it would leak. "Right now, that's all that matters." Unbuckling his seat belt, he glanced at her, waiting. "Now are you coming, or are you planning on spending the night in the Jeep?"

The latter idea thrilled her even less than spending the night in the rickety cabin. With a sigh, Mona pressed the button and undid her seat belt.

"I'm coming, I'm coming," she muttered.

Opening the passenger door, Mona got out. As she stoically battled her way to the cabin's front door, she suddenly shrieked as the cold rain whipped about her face and body, drenching her for a second time in a matter of moments and stealing her breath away, as well.

The next moment, a strong arm tightened around her waist and pulled her the rest of the way to the cabin.

Joe pushed the door open for her. The cabin hadn't had a working lock on it for most of the twenty years it had been empty.

"I can walk," Mona protested as he all but propelled her into the cabin.

"You're welcome," he replied after putting his shoulder to the door and pushing it closed again, despite the fact that the rain seemed to have other ideas.

Steadying herself, Mona scanned the area to get her bearings. The interior of the front room looked particularly dreary, like an old prom dress that had been kept in the closet years too long. The roof, she noted, was leaking in several different spots.

"So much for staying dry," Mona muttered under her breath as she moved aside after a large splotch of rain had hit her on her forehead.

Rubbing his hands together to warm them, Joe gave

her an amused look. "You just have to make sure you don't stand under any of the holes in the roof."

"Brilliant as always." Her voice dripped with sarcasm. "Did you figure that out all by yourself?"

Joe's expression remained stoic and gave nothing away. He deflected the sarcasm with a mild observation as he pointed out, "I'm not the one getting rained on."

Mona struggled with her temper. He wasn't the reason she was in this mood. She'd planned on surprising Rick with her early arrival. He thought she was coming in a couple of weeks, just in time for his wedding. She had sped things up on her end, taking her license exam earlier rather than later, so that she could come and lend a hand in the preparations. Her almost-sister-in-law was six months pregnant and most likely not up to the rigors involved in preparing for a wedding.

Mona knew that a lot of the town was probably willing to pitch in and help, especially Miss Joan who ran the diner and knew everyone's business. But Rick was her only brother, her only family, and she wanted very much to be part of all this. Wanted, she supposed, to be assured that even after the wedding, she would still be a part of his life.

It was all well and good for her to go gallivanting out of town for long spates of time as long as she knew that Rick would be there when she got back. But the thought that he might not be, that he could go off and have a life that didn't directly include her rattled Mona to her very core.

Changing the subject in her attempt to get back on a

more even keel, Mona frowned. She zigzagged across the small room and looked around at her surroundings in the limited light. There was hardly any furniture and what did exist was falling apart.

"Can you imagine living here?" she asked Joe, marveling at the poor quality of life the last inhabitants of the cabin must have had.

"I've seen worse," Joe replied matter-of-factly.

Mona bit her tongue. She could have kicked herself. For a moment, she'd forgotten that he'd spent his early years living on the reservation where poverty and deprivation had been a vivid part of everyday life, not just for Joe, but for everyone there. More than likely, she realized, he'd grown up in a place like this.

She hadn't meant to insult him.

Mona pressed her lips together as she turned to look at him. An apology hovered on her tongue.

"Joe, I didn't mean—"

He didn't want to hear it. Didn't want to glimpse the pity he was certain would come into her eyes, accompanying whatever words would ease her conscience. He wasn't proud of his background, but he wasn't ashamed if it, either. It was what it was. And what it was now was behind him.

Joe waved his hand, dismissing what she was about to say. "Forget it."

Turning his back to her, he focused his attention on the fireplace. Specifically, on making it useful. Squatting down, he angled his head to try to look up the chimney.

Curious, Mona came up behind him. "What are you doing?"

"Trying to see if the chimney's blocked. Last thing you want, if I get a fire going, is to have smoke filling this room." He leaned in a little farther. "Damn," he uttered sharply, pulling back.

Mona moved quickly to get out of his way. "Is it blocked?" she guessed.

"No," he muttered almost grudgingly, "the chimney's clear."

"Okay, I'll bite," she said gamely. "Why are you cursing?"

Disgusted, he rose to his feet for a moment. "Because I wasn't expecting to be hit with big fat raindrops." The last one had been a direct hit into his eye.

Mona laughed. "Especially dirty ones," she observed. He looked at her quizzically. With a flourish, Mona pulled a handkerchief out of the back pocket of her jeans. "Hold still," she ordered.

"Why?" he asked suspiciously. Mona was nothing if not unpredictable. Added to that she had a wicked sense of humor.

"Because I can't hit a moving target," she deadpanned, then said seriously, "Because I want to wipe the dirt off your face." Doing so in gentle strokes, she shook her head. "God, but you've gotten to be really distrusting since I was last home."

"No, I haven't," he protested.

Saying that, he took the handkerchief from her and wiped his own face. He told himself it was in the interest of efficiency and that reacting to the way she stroked his face with the handkerchief had nothing to do with it. Some lies, he argued, were necessary, even if they were transparent.

"I never trusted you in the first place." He raised his chin a little, presenting his face for Mona's scrutiny. "Did I get it all?"

"Why ask me?" she asked innocently. "After all, I could be lying."

"True," he agreed, "but seeing as how you're the only one around this cabin besides me who talks, I have no choice. You'll have to do."

"You look fine," she told him, playfully running her index finger down his cheek. "You got it all, Deputy Lone Wolf."

He held out the handkerchief to her. "Thanks." When she took it from him, Joe turned his attention back to the fireplace and getting a fire going. There was kindling beside the stone fireplace. It didn't appear to be that old. Someone had obviously been here and used the fireplace since the last owner had vacated the premises. He shifted several pieces, positioning them in the hearth.

Mona went over to the lone window that faced the front of the house and looked out. The rain seemed to be coming down even harder, if that was possible. She shivered slightly, not so much from the cold as from the feeling of isolation.

"Think this'll last all night?" she asked Joe, still staring out the window.

He hefted another log, putting it on top of the others. "That's what they say."

She didn't like the sound of that. Turning away from the window, she addressed her words to his back. "You mean, we have to stay here until morning?"

Joe fished a book of matches out of his front pocket.

He didn't smoke anymore, hadn't for years now, but he still liked to have a book of matches in his possession. You never knew when they might come in handy—like now. He had no patience with the old ways when it came to making fire, even though, when push came to shove, he was good at it.

"Unless you want to risk being caught in a flash flood the way we almost were back there."

She sighed, moving about restlessly. The cabin was sinking into darkness and although she'd grown up in Forever, this setup was disquieting.

"Not exactly the way I pictured spending my first night back home," she told him.

"You mean, stranded and hungry?" he guessed.

"For openers," she agreed. Mona ran her hand along her extremely flat abdomen. It had been rumbling for a while now.

He crossed to her. It might have been her imagination, but Joe seemed somehow taller to her in this cabin.

"When did you eat last?" he wanted to know.

"This morning. I skipped lunch to get an early start driving down to Forever." It had seemed like a good idea at the time. She hadn't bothered to listen to the weather forecast. She wished she had now. "I figured I'd be in time to grab a late lunch at Miss Joan's," she added. Miss Joan, the owner of the diner, had been a fixture around Forever for as long as she could remember.

Arms wrapped around her to ward off the chill, Mona glanced around the cabin's main room again. "Doesn't look as if there's been food around here for a good long while."

"Except for maybe the four-footed kind," Joe interjected as the sound of something small and swift was heard rustling toward the rear of the room. A rat?

"I'll pass, thanks," she muttered. She wasn't *that* hungry yet, Mona thought. She preferred meals that *didn't* deliver themselves.

"You sure?" Joe asked, a hint of a grin on his lips. "I hear that squirrels and possums taste just like—"

"Chicken, yes, I've heard the same myth," she said, cutting him off. "I'll let you know if I get that hungry. I'm not there yet." And hopefully never would be, she added silently.

He looked mildly amused. "Suit yourself."

"What, you're willing to eat a squirrel?" she challenged. He couldn't be serious, she thought. Joe knew better than that. "They're full of diseases. You won't have any idea what you're swallowing," she insisted.

"Yeah, I will," he said.

Was he just trying to bait her? And then she realized that Joe was walking toward the door. He couldn't be going out—or could he? "Where are you going?" she wanted to know.

"To my Jeep to get the dinner I was bringing home from Miss Joan's."

"You had food all this time and you let me go on about the rodents?" she demanded.

"Never known anyone to be able to stop you once you got wound up," he pointed out. "I figured I'd just wait it out, like the storm. Be right back," he told her. He opened the door only as much as he had to in order to slip out.

He heard her muttering a few choice words aimed in his direction before the wind carried them away.

Making his way to the Jeep, Joe smiled to himself. Yup, same old Mona. There was a comfort in that.

Chapter Three

Wind and rain accompanied Joe's reentry into the cabin several minutes later. Mona was quick to throw her weight against the door in order to shut it again.

"Took you long enough," she commented, hoping to divert his attention from the fact that she had been right next to the door, waiting for his return. Her concern had nothing to do with hunger. But there was no way she was about to admit that.

"I'll move faster next time." Opening his jacket, he took out the prize and placed it on the rickety kitchen table. The next moment, he shed the jacket and spread it out in front of the fireplace. With any luck, it would be dry by morning.

"Any sign of the storm breaking up?" she asked hopefully. She really wanted to be in town before nightfall.

Joe shook his head. "If anything, it's getting worse," he told her.

Frowning, Mona glanced at the food he'd braved the elements to bring in.

"This is all that you eat?" she asked incredulously.

The only thing on the table was a roast-beef sandwich, perched on a bed of wax paper.

"I wasn't planning on having to share it with anyone," Joe said a little defensively.

"Share?" she repeated. "It's not big enough for one person, let alone two." The man was six-two with a far better than average build. Didn't that take some kind of decent fuel to maintain? "Don't you get hungry?"

Wide, strong shoulders rose and then fell carelessly beneath his deputy's shirt. The material strained against his biceps.

"Not really," he answered. "Eating's never been a big deal for me."

It wasn't exactly a new revelation. Thinking back, she knew that no one could ever accuse Joe of consuming too much. He's always had the build of a rock-hard athlete without so much as an ounce of fat to spare. It was the reason that so many girls drooled over him. Or at least one of the reasons, she amended. The fact that he had brooding good looks didn't exactly hurt.

Joe didn't sit down at the table. Instead, he pushed the sandwich toward her. "You can have most of it if you like. I'm not really hungry."

Well, she was. While tempted to take him at his word, Mona didn't really believe him. He was just being Joe and that entailed being quietly noble. She wasn't about to take advantage of that. Hungry or not, it didn't seem fair.

"When did *you* last eat?" she asked him, repeating the question that Joe had put to her less than a few minutes ago.

He didn't even bother trying to remember, shrugging

off the question. "I don't know." He made a vague gesture with his hand. "I don't live by a clock when it comes to food. I eat when I'm hungry, I don't when I'm not."

"We'll split it," she declared, her tone saying that she wasn't about to take no for an answer and she was done discussing it. Gingerly sitting down on one of the two chairs, Mona picked up the half closest to her.

Joe ignored the finality in her tone. "You just said that there wasn't even enough for one person," he reminded her.

Was he *trying* to pick a fight? Mona forced a fake smile to her lips. "And now I'm saying that we're splitting it. Seems to me if you can listen to me say one thing, you can listen to me say the other."

He laughed shortly and picked up the half closest to him. "It's been dull without you here."

She took a bite and savored it before commenting on his statement. Miss Joan's food was plain, but it could always be counted on to be delicious. "I don't think my brother would agree, what with finding first a baby, then the baby's aunt on his doorstep."

"Technically, the baby's aunt turned up on the diner's doorstep," Joe corrected just before he took his first bite of the sandwich.

Mona looked at him. She'd known that. Rick had given her all the details—after she'd pressed him for them—when he called to tell her he was getting married. For the purpose of narrative, she'd exaggerated. She should have known better around Joe.

"I forgot what a real stickler for details you could be."

"Gotta pay attention to the facts," he pointed out

mildly. "Without the facts, your story can turn into someone else's."

Too tired to unscramble his remark, she took another healthy bite of her half, but needed something to wash it down with.

"You wouldn't happen to have brought along a beverage with your 'dinner,' would you?" she asked.

"I've got beer at home," he told her.

"Doesn't exactly do us any good here, now does it?"

Setting what was left of her half down on the wax paper, Mona eased herself off the chair, taking care not to make any sudden movements that might cause the legs to separate from the seat.

Meanwhile Joe had made his way over to the sink and slowly turned the faucet. It squealed in protest just before the water emerged. The smell alone was terrible. The color was a close second.

He turned off the faucet. "Well, water's out unless rust is your favorite flavor."

Since he was conducting the search, she sank back down on her chair. Her half of the sandwich was disappearing much too quickly, she thought, silently lamenting that he hadn't brought two.

"I'll pass." She watched Joe as he opened and then closed the overhead cabinets. "Anything?"

He was about to say "No," but the last cabinet he opened contained an old, half-empty bottle of whiskey. Judging from the dust, it had been left behind a long time ago.

Turning back to face her, he held the bottle aloft. "Does this count?"

"Rot-gut," Mona cried, using the word that had defined crudely made alcohol a couple of centuries ago. That wouldn't have been her first choice, but any port in a storm, she reasoned. "It'll do in a pinch."

"We're going to have to drink straight out of the bottle," he told her, crossing back to Mona and placing the bottle in the middle of the table. "Seems like the last owner didn't believe in glasses." His eyes briefly met hers. "I can't find any."

Mona scrutinized the bottle. The light from the fireplace bathed it with gentle strokes, making it gleam amber. But there was no missing the thick dust. She hesitated. "Think it's safe to drink?" she asked him.

"Only one way to find out," Joe answered gamely. Before Mona could say anything further, he tilted the bottle back and took a small swig. Even that little bit jolted him. It took him a couple of seconds to find his breath. "Hell of a kick," he told her.

Suddenly, Joe grabbed his chest and began making strangling noises. His eyes rolled back in his head. Horrified, Mona was instantly on her feet. Throwing her arms around him, she struggled to lower him to the floor. She needed to get him to a flat surface before she could start CPR.

Mona did her best to fight back panic. "Joe, talk to me, what do you feel? Can you breathe? Damn it, you shouldn't have—"

The words dried up on her tongue when she caught a glimpse of Joe's face. He wasn't choking, he was laughing.

Furious, she opened her arms and his upper torso dropped, hitting the floor with a thud.

"Idiot!" she bit off. "I thought you were poisoned." She crossed her arms before her angrily. "I should have known the poison hadn't been invented that could do away with you."

Getting up off the floor, Joe dusted himself off. "A second ago, you were worried that I was dying. Now you're mad that I'm not. You sure do blow hot and cold, don't you?" he asked with a laugh.

Mona frowned as she sat down at the table again. For a moment, she said nothing, just ate the rest of her sandwich in silence.

He supposed it was a dirty trick. Sitting down opposite her, he apologized. Sort of. It would have carried more weight if he wasn't grinning. "Sorry, I just couldn't resist."

She raised her eyes to his face, glaring at him. "That was a rotten trick."

"Yes, it was," he responded solemnly. She knew he was just humoring her.

"So? How is it?" she pressed, changing the subject. When he looked at her quizzically, she nodded at the bottle on the table. "The whiskey."

"Pretty smooth for rot-gut," he told her. When he saw her reaching for the bottle, he advised, "Go slow if you're going to try it."

He realized his mistake the moment the words were out of his mouth.

"The day I can't hold my liquor as well as you can is the day I'll admit myself into a nursing home and spend the rest of my days sitting in a rocking chair in a corner—rocking."

He didn't crack a smile. "There is middle ground, you know."

"Not for people like you and me," she told him just before she took a swig from the bottle, determined to match him.

Joe watched her eyes tear up as the whiskey hit bottom. He knew better than to laugh, or even point the fact out. That would only goad her on. For all her education, she really hadn't changed that much, he mused. She still had that sharp, competitive edge that made her see everything as a personal challenge, even when it wasn't.

She would have never made it as a Navajo, he thought. The Native American tribe was known for *not* competing. They saw competing against their fellow man as being impolite.

Mona had never been hampered by those kinds of feelings.

"How is it?" he asked, infusing just enough disinterest in his voice to sound believable.

"Smooth, like you said," she managed to get out, her voice a raspy whisper. It felt as if the whiskey had instantly stripped her vocal cords, but she wasn't about to let on. Mona deliberately took another swig.

Liquid flames poured through her body. Even so, this time it was a little less jarring than the first sip she'd taken.

He wanted to tell her not to overdo it, but he knew better. Mona was nothing if not contrary. When she set the bottle down, the look in her eyes wasn't hard to read. She dared him to take another swig himself.

So he did.

And then it was her turn again. Joe caught himself thinking that he was grateful the pint bottle was half empty when they found it. The damage caused by the whiskey wouldn't be too great.

Worst case, Mona would get light-headed and giddy for a bit, but since she was with him, she was safe.

Lucky for her, Joe thought rather grudgingly.

Yeah, you're a regular Boy Scout, aren't you?

The bottle was passed back and forth between them, traveling faster with each handoff. Before either one of them realized it, nothing was left.

With a sigh, Mona tilted the bottle all the way over, trying to coax another drop out, but without success.

She felt oddly relaxed and revved up at the same time, as if sliding around in a bright, shiny echo chamber.

Setting the bottle down on its side, she planted her hands on the tabletop and pushed herself up into a standing position. The chair behind her fell. There was a crash accompanied by a cracking sound as parts splintered against the floor.

Mona glanced behind her, mildly surprised. "Oops," she murmured. "Don't make them like they used to, do they?" Drawing herself up to her full height, she turned to her left a bit too quickly and found herself wavering unsteadily on her feet.

The sudden action had intensified her dizziness. "I think the wind is pushing the room around," she told Joe just before she tilted too far to the right.

Jumping to his feet quickly, Joe managed to grab her before Mona could fall over. "Guess that must be it," he agreed.

Her eyes narrowed as she forgot what had brought her to her feet to begin with.

"What are you doing over here? You were just over there." She pointed to his chair as if it was located on the other side of town.

"Wind blew me over here, too." He figured she'd accept that, thinking that if the wind was responsible for moving the room around, it could just as easily have moved him, too.

He should have known better.

Grabbing the front of his shirt with her hands in an effort to really steady herself—or the room—Mona stared up into his face rather intently. "Know what I think?" she asked him.

The woman was entirely too close to him, Joe thought. Her sweet breath mingled with the distinct scent of the whiskey she'd consumed, creating a very odd combination that reeled him in. He was acutely aware of every single supple inch of her. As well as his own body. Struggling, he did his best to appear indifferent.

He wasn't, but in her present state, he hoped Mona wouldn't notice. If she pressed up against him, all bets were off.

"What?" he finally asked her.

She was really trying to focus and not doing an overly good job of it. "I think that you're trying to take advantage of me, Joe."

That was when she moved in closer to him, as if that could somehow help her read him better. She pressed all her curves against the hard contours of his body and in turn threatened to create Joe's own personal meltdown.

"Are you trying to take advantage of me?" Mona asked.

He did his best to try to make her turn toward the rear of the cabin. Hands ever so lightly on her shoulders, he maneuvered her toward it. "Right now, I think you should lie down. There's a bed in the other room."

"Ah-ha! I was right. I knew it," Mona declared triumphantly, swinging around so that she could grasp hold of his shirtfront again, crumpling it beneath her fingers. "You *are* trying to take advantage of me. Oh, Joe—"

Every fiber of his being wanted to give in, but he continued to fight it. "No, I'm—"

The rest of his adamant protest went unspoken. He found it impossible to speak when Mona's lips were suddenly and firmly pressed against his.

She was quick, he'd give her that.

She was also damn intoxicating, far more potent than an old, half-empty bottle of aged whiskey, Joe caught himself thinking—while he could still think.

But that ability quickly faded as the taste of Mona's lips steadily got to him, weakening his resolve. Making him want Mona with a fierceness that jarred him.

The will to push her away, to do the right thing, was not nearly as strong as it should have been. As strong as it had been only moments ago.

His lips worked over hers, deepening the kiss.

He tasted her moan and felt the blood surge through his veins as if it had been set on fire.

Maybe it had been.

He needed to put a stop to this.

In a moment. Just one more moment.

He promised himself that he would do the right thing in a moment. Right now, just for this erotic half a heartbeat, he wanted to enjoy this completely unexpected turn of events.

Wanted to enjoy the feel of her warm body pressed so urgently against his.

Wanted to savor the taste of her mouth as it drained his soul away. With the least bit of encouragement, he would have fallen to his knees, silently begging her for more.

But that wasn't going to happen for a whole host of reasons, not the least of which was pride.

His.

So, realizing that this was a once-in-a-lifetime occurrence, like Halley's Comet, he took his time ending it.

Took full enjoyment of the moment—and her.

The very act, even as it was occurring, left him vulnerable, unmasking the secret that he had tried to keep, even from himself. That he wanted this woman with the laughing eyes and the sinful mouth. Had always wanted her and would, most likely, go to his grave wanting her.

In silence.

Because a man had his pride and any admission as to the depth and breadth of his feelings—his *unrequited* feelings—for Mona would expose him and leave him open to ridicule and pity, neither one of which he could endure.

With a jolt, Joe realized that he was very close to

the edge of the vortex. To the point of no return. Any second now, it would suck him in, rendering him a prisoner of this feeling and leaving him incapable of cutting off this kiss.

Incapable of walking away.

He already didn't want to. Fiercely.

If he didn't back away in a moment, there would *be* no backing away. Because he was only a man, only flesh and blood, and his flesh and blood craved hers.

Now! Stop it now! Before you can't!

Inflamed, Joe went on kissing her.

And she was kissing him back just as urgently.

Chapter Four

The sound of her own groan rudely nudged Mona into semiwakefulness.

An elephant tap-danced on her head. A heavy elephant that threatened to crush her skull any second now.

Mona curled up into herself, trying to hide from the creature, from the pain that his lumbering movements created.

But there was nowhere to hide.

As the haze lifted, scraping slowly along her awakening consciousness, she realized that she was squeezing her eyes shut. Squeezing them shut in self-defense.

Why?

Was she afraid of seeing something? Someone?

Very cautiously, Mona pried her eyelids open. The moment she did, she instantly shut them again.

The sunlight hurt her head.

Sunlight?

Her eyes popped open and she jackknifed up into a sitting position. The pain doubled but she valiantly struggled to ignore it as urgent messages telegraphed themselves to her throbbing brain.

The incessant, heavy rain had stopped. As had the moaning wind. The world was still.

She was on a striped, bare mattress that smelled as if it had been used every day for the past two centuries, all without being cleaned.

She'd gotten drunk, she suddenly recalled.

Drunk with Joe.

Joe! *Omigod, Joe!*

Shock raced through her aching mind as bits and pieces of last night came back to her, jumbled and completely out of order. The only thing she specifically remembered was throwing herself at him.

Hard.

And then nothing.

She covered her mouth in growing agitation. She couldn't remember what happened after she'd hermetically sealed her mouth to his.

Had he—

Had they—

"Oh, God," Mona groaned more loudly this time as her distress mounted. She dragged her hand through her hair. The roots hurt. Her skull hurt.

Did that mean that she…?

That he…?

"Oh, God," Mona groaned again, confused, embarrassed and absolutely, unequivocally miserable.

"He's busy. Will I do in a pinch?" Joe asked.

The sound of her groaning voice had drawn him in. The expression on her face as she looked up at him told him everything he needed to know. She remembered last night.

That made two of them.

"You—you—" She couldn't bring herself to finish the sentence, hoping against hope that nothing had happened. Afraid that it had. And worse, not knowing how to bluff her way through this to get him to tell her the details—or the lack of any—without admitting that there was a huge void in her aching brain.

"It stopped raining," Joe informed her mildly as if he hadn't noticed her sudden inability to form a complete, coherent sentence. "Hell, it looks as if it never even rained at all." There were only a few small puddles to hint at the rising waters that had encroached around the cabin yesterday. "I can get you into town now."

And then, because he wasn't entirely a plastered saint and because he couldn't resist teasing her just a little, he stood in the doorway of the tiny bedroom where he'd deposited her passed-out body last night and grinned wickedly at her.

"Unless, of course, you'd rather stay here for a while longer...." His voice trailed off, leaving the rest to her imagination.

Mona instantly stiffened. Something *had* happened last night. "No, I don't want to stay here a second longer," she informed him woodenly, scrambling off the sagging, weathered mattress. "Not *one* second longer."

Feet planted firmly on the floor, her head still throbbing like a war drum pressed into use, Mona raised her chin pugnaciously, ready to go toe to toe with him in order to get at the truth.

"What happened last night, Joe?"

The wicked grin remained. "You weren't yourself," he answered.

There were *so* many different ways to take that, and from where she stood, none of them were good. "Exactly who *was* I?" she demanded.

Enjoying himself, Joe played it out a little longer. He turned on his heel, ready to leave the room and the cabin. "Maybe we'd better leave that to another time." He kept his voice deliberately vague.

He figured she owed him, seeing as how he'd been the personification of honorableness last night. Turning a deaf ear to the demands that his body fairly shouted at him.

Stunned that he wasn't answering her, Mona launched herself at the doorway, making it half a step before he reached it. Hands on either side of the doorjamb, trying not to wince from the pain in her head, Mona blocked his way.

"Maybe we better not," she countered. Damn but her head was killing her. Any sudden movement on her part just intensified the crushing pounding. "*What* happened?" she asked again, enunciating each word slowly, her teeth clenched.

Silent, Joe watched her for a long moment. She didn't remember anything. Hadn't witnessed his superhuman struggles with himself to finally separate her lips from his and hold her at arm's length. Didn't remember that she'd pushed his hands away and snuggled up against him again, her soft, inviting body promising him a time he wouldn't soon forget—and she wouldn't remember.

That had been just the trouble. Whether it was just the liquor talking, or the liquor dissolving the inhibitions that kept her from him, he didn't know. What he did know was that if he made love with a woman, she would damn well be conscious of her decision to meet him halfway, not slide to meet him on a slick path of mind-numbing alcohol.

"Nothing happened," he finally said.

If it was nothing, then why had it taken him so long to say the word? And why couldn't she remember anything beyond—

Oh, God, she'd kissed him.

Kissed him? She'd all but swallowed his mouth up whole, she realized as the memory came vividly crashing back to her, heating her blood at the same time. Heating all of her.

Embarrassed, Mona could feel her cheeks suddenly blazing. It took everything she had not to try to cover them up with her hands.

She tried diversion. "Don't lie to me," she snapped angrily.

His eyes captured hers, making a soul-to-soul connection, the way he used to back when he would walk her home from school and dreams were cheap.

"When have you ever known me to lie?" he asked her quietly.

Mona shrugged, struggling to recapture the dignity she felt she'd forfeited by allowing her old, and secret, girlhood crush on Joe to come out last night.

"For the most part, I've been gone these past eight years." Although she had come home almost every summer. "I don't know. You could have changed."

But even as she said it, Mona knew she didn't really believe that.

"I didn't," he replied flatly.

"So what did happen after I glued my mouth to yours?"

"You passed out."

Mona froze inside. This was worse than she'd thought. No wonder she didn't remember anything. She wasn't conscious for it. "And then what?" she asked in a quiet voice.

"And then I carried you into this room and put you to bed," he told her matter-of-factly.

"And?" she asked, her voice hitching in her throat as she waited for the rest of the details. Joe never said all that much, but he had a way of stringing it out, and right now, he drove her crazy. It was hard not to let her irritation just jump out at him.

"And I slept on the couch."

Mona drew in a shaky breath, trying to do it quietly. Was he really saying nothing happened? "And that's all?" she questioned.

"That's all." He cocked his head. "Why, what else did you want to have happen?" he asked innocently.

"Want?" she repeated indignantly. Did Joe suspect that she'd had feelings for him? No, how could he? She'd never given him any reason to suspect—until last night, she thought ruefully. "Nothing. Absolutely nothing," Mona retorted with emphasis.

One dark eyebrow arched higher than the other. "That why you kissed me, Mona?"

"I didn't kiss you!" Mona shot back. And then, because he was grinning at her knowingly, and because she actually *had* kissed him, she added, "Like you said, that wasn't me."

"Sure looked like you," he told her.

He got a real kick out of watching her squirm. Since he'd played the noble guy while everything inside of him screamed not to allow this one once-in-a-lifetime opportunity slip through his fingers, she owed him a little entertainment at her expense. After all, he'd been noble even though it had cost him.

Joe had taken off her boots, she noted, grabbing them from the floor. Going out into the main room, she hobbled over to the sofa. Overall, she was grateful to him, but right now, the humiliation of her unscheduled transformation into a passion-laced woman haunted her and she wanted nothing more than to divert his attention from that image.

Planting herself on the sofa so she could pull on her boots, she addressed Joe in a clipped voice, "Can we just get going?"

He nodded. "The rain didn't sweep away the Jeep, so whenever you're ready, we're good to go."

Boots on, she jumped up to her feet. "Ready," she announced. The next moment she winced again from the pain shooting through her temples.

"Bad?" he asked sympathetically.

"What do you think?" She eyed him accusingly. They had both had the same amount to drink last night, that much she remembered. So why wasn't his head splitting in two like hers was? "Why didn't that whiskey affect you?"

"Oh, it did," he told her, thinking of how his resistance to her had been lowered. Had the whiskey not affected him, he wouldn't have let things go as far as they had. If nothing else, his background had taught him how to stoically do without. Not having her was part of that. "I just handle it better."

Had she not been feeling sick, she would have taken that as a challenge to her own capabilities when it came to tolerating alcohol. But that was a catch-22 situation, she thought. So she said nothing as she lowered herself into the passenger seat and buckled up.

The less said, she decided, the less her head hurt, and right now, that was all that counted.

IT DIDN'T TAKE THAT LONG to get into the heart of Forever. Joe made the decision to go there instead of stopping at the house that Mona shared with her brother. He'd already gathered that her main purpose was to see Rick first, and at this hour, the sheriff was most likely in his office.

The additional benefit of going straight to town was that he could get Mick moving. The sooner he got the mechanic to tow in her vehicle and fix the flat, the sooner life would begin to get back to normal for Mona, he reasoned.

As for him, well, the memory of last night and what had *almost* gone down would linger in his mind for a very long time, as would the revelation that, just as he'd always believed, her lips had tasted incredibly sweet. That, too, would have to sustain him for an indefinite period to come. He knew there would be no replays, instant or otherwise.

Joe brought the Jeep to a halt before the sheriff's building, parking it in the only space still available. Turning off the ignition and pulling up the hand brake, he was surprised that Mona remained beside him. He'd expected her to hop out. Under ordinary circumstances, he'd have to grab her to keep her inside the vehicle until it stopped moving.

"Something wrong?" he asked her.

Mona sat looking straight ahead, as if debating answering or just quietly getting out of the vehicle.

With a suppressed sigh, she turned toward him and said, "I'm sorry if I took your head off back there."

The apology was even a greater surprise than her silence. He wondered what was going in her head. To his recollection, Mona had never been the type to tender her apologies.

She would have to have gone a long way before she measured up to anything he'd endured after his mother had died, leaving his welfare up in the air and at the mercy of a host of relatives who all had better things to do than raise a homeless boy.

"You didn't," he told her.

Mona knew better. She'd been rude and short with him and none of it had really been his fault. But she was trying to work certain things out in her head and, through no fault of his own, he had been a handy target.

"And about last night…" She wanted him to know that it wasn't the thought of being with him that had horrified her this morning. It was the idea of not remembering, of believing that she hadn't had control over her actions.

"There's nothing to talk about," Joe told her. Nothing had happened beyond the one soul-searing kiss and she didn't need to agonize over and regret. They would continue the way they always had, as more than friends, less than lovers. "Now, why don't you go inside and see your brother before someone does start talking about you sitting out here with me in my Jeep?"

Other than playing poker, gossip and rumors were the number one diversion for a lot of the citizens of Forever. She didn't want to give them any more fuel than they probably already felt they had. She was in no mood to be forgiving right now and probably wouldn't be until she'd worked out what was bothering her.

"Right."

Unbuckling her seat belt, Mona got out of the vehicle. The heels of her boots made rhythmic, staccato sounds as they hit the pavement before the short, squat office's front door.

She didn't bother knocking before she entered. The door was unlocked, which meant that at least one of the four-man team was in.

From the sound of it, the entire crew was present except, of course, for Joe, who for some reason hadn't followed her in. She didn't have time to wonder why.

The first to see her was Alma Rodriquez. Glancing up from her desk, the slender, dark-haired deputy was on her feet, running across the room to Mona with her arms outstretched. The next second, Mona found herself caught up in a fierce hug. For a small woman, Alma was exceptionally strong. She'd said it had something to do with growing up with five brothers and trying to hold her own.

"Hey, Mona, what are you doing here?" Alma cried, her voice muffled against Mona's shoulder. "Rick told me that you weren't coming in until the day before his and Olivia's wedding."

Mona hugged the woman back, partially in self-defense to keep from being smothered and partially because Alma, Larry and Joe were family to her. Coming to the office felt more like a home to her than the house where she'd grown up. Without her grandmother there and with Rick at work, the old building just felt like a shell with memories.

She pushed aside the sudden pang that sought to entangle her.

"I decided you guys needed my help getting everything ready," Mona told her with a laugh.

Alma released Mona only to have her place taken by Larry Collins, the third deputy. Older than Joe or Alma, the tall, blond-haired man treated Mona as if she was *his* little sister and not the sheriff's.

"Good to see you, little girl," he said with feeling, stepping back. He smiled at Mona appreciatively. "You just keep getting prettier every time I see you. Good thing you came early. With you around, the sheriff's fiancée can get to see that there's a pretty side to his family after all."

"What the hell's all this noise?" Rick asked, coming out of his office. "It sure better have something to do with seeing to all the damage caused by yesterday's flash flood—"

Rick stopped talking when Mona swung around to face him. Grinning, she threw up her hands like a gymnast jumping off the uneven bars after completing her program, waiting for applause.

"Surprise."

Rick's mouth dropped open. His sister was two weeks early. "Mona, what the hell are you doing here?"

"Surviving being hugged by your deputies," she deadpanned as she crossed over to him. And then she answered him seriously, leaving out the part that a sense of anxiety had prompted her to come early. That was her problem to work out, not his. "I decided that I wanted to be more than just a spectator at my only brother's wedding."

Because he was glad to see her, alive and well and in one piece, he paused to hug her. Then stepped back, as all the things that could have happened to her took over his thoughts. A disapproving look mingled with the deep love for his younger sister.

"You should have waited until I came up for you." That had been the plan, for him to fetch her and bring her down here the day before the wedding. They'd left it at that, with her agreeing. He should have known better. Mona was far too impetuous for her own good. "You know how I feel about you driving at night. Especially in a storm," he emphasized.

"I didn't drive through the night—or the storm," she told him. "When I left Dallas, it wasn't raining. I stopped when it started getting bad." For now, she left out the part about the flat. No sense in giving her overprotective brother more ammunition.

His eyes narrowed. "Where'd you stop?"

She sighed, shaking her head. When she looked to Alma for help, the woman conveniently retreated to her work. She was on her own here.

"Do you have to play twenty questions now?" she asked her brother. "I haven't even been here two minutes. The least you can do is pretend like you're happy to see me."

"I *am* happy to see you, you know that." But he pinned her down with a look, the way he'd seen his grandmother do more than once. The old woman had been the only one who had ever managed to make his sister toe the line. "I'm just curious how you managed to avoid getting caught in the storm."

"She didn't avoid it," Joe said, aware that all eyes turned toward him as he walked into the office. He'd stopped by Mick's garage and given the mechanic directions as to where to find Mona's Jeep. Mick had put the sheriff's sister up to the head of his list and taken off before any of the other customers he had coming in today could complain. "Mona spent the night at the old Murphy place halfway between the reservation and town."

"I *know* where the old Murphy place is," Rick told him.

"That moth-eaten old cabin?" Alma cried in surprise, then looked at Mona. "You poor thing. What a way to spend your first night back."

Rick had a more important question. He addressed it to Joe. "How would you know about that?"

"'Cause I was there, too," Joe told him.

Crossing over to his desk, he acted as if he didn't know that he'd just detonated a major bomb right in the middle of the room.

Without pausing to stop, Joe picked up his mug, which was in desperate need of cleaning, and went to make himself some coffee. Ordinarily, he wasn't awake before the first cup. But today, watching Mona sleep had done a lot to get his blood moving.

Still, he had a feeling he was going to need more. He usually wasn't wrong when it came to feelings.

Chapter Five

Mona saw the look that entered her brother's green eyes as they shifted from her to Joe and then back again. She could almost hear the thoughts and questions sprouting like weeds in his mind. Thank God he didn't know anything about the bottle of whiskey they'd found. Or the kiss.

"Don't go all 'big brother' on me, Rick," she warned. "If it wasn't for Joe, I would probably have been swept away to who knows where," she informed her brother. "Joe came to my rescue."

Ordinarily an easygoing, laid-back sort of a man, all sorts of protective instincts rose to the fore when it came to his sister. Subconsciously, he always felt he had to step in for the father who had died before she was even a year old.

Rick took her answer with more than a degree of skepticism. "Oh? Would either one of you care to elaborate how this rescue wound up with you two spending the night together in the old Murphy cabin?"

Coffee mug in hand, Joe crossed back to the sheriff. All eyes were now on him. Stoically, he recited the facts as if he'd just been sworn in on the witness stand. "Her

Jeep's front right tire was flat—so was her spare. I was on my way home, saw her cursing at the tire and offered to take her back to town. The storm was getting worse and visibility next to impossible, so when we drove by the cabin, I decided it was better if we just waited it out there instead of running the risk of getting caught in a flash flood."

"So you picked the cozy cabin," Rick interjected, his tone far from satisfied.

"Cozy?" The incredulous utterance came from Alma, who hooted at the very thought of what her boss was suggesting. "Hell, Rick, have you *seen* that cabin lately? Not even a raccoon in heat would call it 'cozy.' Staying there's like spending the night in a Dumpster."

"How would you know that?" Larry asked, curious.

"That's not the point here," Alma pointed out evasively.

The cabin hadn't been that bad, Joe thought, taking a deep sip of his coffee. But for the sake of putting Rick's mind at ease, he decided it best to keep his observation to himself.

For a moment, it looked as if the sheriff would subject them to more probing questions. But then, mercifully, Rick shrugged, letting the matter drop

He nodded toward Alma. "Yeah, I guess you're right. Nobody would willingly spend the night in that place."

Her brother might be willing to let the matter drop, but Mona wasn't. She took umbrage with his line of questioning.

"Alma might be right," Mona allowed, "but you seem to be forgetting that I'm twenty-six." She saw Rick's eyebrows narrow, as sure sign that he wasn't pleased with what he was hearing, but she pressed on. He had to be made to respect her as an adult, not a child. "Don't you think it's about time you stopped acting as if I was fifteen and still needed someone to guard my virtue?"

"Time to get back to work," Larry announced loudly, turning away and clearly indicating that he had no intentions of taking sides in what looked to be a possible war between his boss and Mona.

Alma took her cue from Larry and glanced at her watch. "My turn to go on patrol," she said to no one in particular.

Strapping on her sidearm and picking up her hat, the petite woman was out the door before any more words were exchanged.

Rick stood there for a moment as if debating two lines of thought. Coming to a conclusion, he turned to Joe. "Sorry, Joe. I should have just thanked you for bringing her in safely."

Joe brushed off any real need for an apology. "That's okay."

She wasn't exactly thrilled with that wording, either. All she wanted was to be treated as an equal, not an afterthought that needed special tending.

"Bringing me in safely?" Mona asked, incensed. "What am I, a stray mare to be 'brought in safely'?"

Rick allowed a smile to curve his mouth. "No, definitely not a mare. Mares can be gentled. You're more like a burr under a mustang's saddle."

Mona decided to take his comment as a compliment and smiled.

Though a great deal more vulnerable than anyone suspected—or possibly because of it—she'd made a point of never coming across as meek and mild. The meek and mild were stepped on and pushed around on a regular basis.

"Now that that's out of the way," Mona said, the edge gone from her voice, "you have any aspirin around here, Rick?" she asked hopefully. "My head's about to split open."

"Why didn't you say so earlier?" Rick asked. "I've got a whole bottle of the stuff in my office." Leading the way back, he grinned. "I stocked up when I knew you were coming home."

"Very funny," she retorted. But there was affection in her voice as she said it. And a smile bloomed on her face when he put his arm around her shoulders, guiding her into his glass-walled office.

"BE WITH YOU IN A MINUTE," Dr. Henry Whitmore, affectionately referred to as "Doc" by everyone who knew him, called out from the back room. His words were addressed to whoever had just walked into the front of his clinic, setting off a series of chimes that corresponded to the beginning notes of "How Much Is That Doggie in the Window?" He'd had the chimes ever since he'd opened his animal hospital in Forever more than thirty years ago.

There was something incredibly comforting in hearing the chimes, Mona thought as she walked in. It connected her to her childhood and all the years she'd spent here, apprenticing Doc, learning from experience what no textbooks could have possibly conveyed nearly so well.

From the time she was eleven until she went off to college, Doc's animal hospital had been like another home to her. She'd felt comfortable here. Useful. And so in her element. She couldn't always communicate with people, her emotions getting in the way. But animals were a different story. She had an affinity for animals. And they responded to her in kind, as if sensing the compassion she had for them, the respect with which she regarded all of them.

She'd loved animals ever since she could remember. Animals were loyal. If you showed them affection, they stayed. They didn't just take off one morning, promising to be back but never meaning to keep their word, the way her mother had.

Her grandmother had solemnly called her an animal whisperer. The old woman had said that this was her calling. Her "gift." It was obvious that animals seemed to be attracted to her. She could get them to do things that other people couldn't. Mona was gentle with them, patient, and they trusted her even when they were sick or hurt.

She decided early on that her mission in life was to help these creatures that looked at her so trustingly, to make them well and to generally improve their quality of life. Because she was so determined to help every sick animal she found, it was only natural that her path would cross with Doc's. From the time she was a little girl, he took a special interest in her and invited her to his clinic to be his "assistant."

In time, she actually became one. She worked for him after school and on weekends. She would have done it for free just to be around the animals, but he insisted on paying her. Told her to save the money for her schooling, which she did, religiously.

That was how her college fund initially got started. Even so, it still wouldn't have been enough for more than a year's worth of tuition and expenses if Doc hadn't come through again.

He insisted on giving her the money she needed to fund the rest of her education. Never married and childless, with no known relatives, Doc told Mona that she was the daughter he would have wanted to have if things had worked out differently for him. At the time he'd told her, she had the feeling that he'd loved someone once who hadn't return that affection, but he never elaborated any further and she didn't pry.

What she did do was promise to pay him back as soon as she was able. He'd answered that he wasn't worried about getting his money back. He considered what he was doing to be a sound investment.

After her brother, Doc was the first person she went to see after she got into town.

Henry Whitmore came out of the back room where he performed his surgeries as well as his examinations on the smaller animals brought in either as beloved pets or wounded strays. He saw them all and treated them all. No animal was turned away because of the owner's inability to pay. Neither did he turn out the strays. In his book, a suffering creature needed to be helped. It was as simple as that for him.

Gray-haired with deep blue eyes, Doc was a robust-looking man in his late fifties. He wore his glasses on the tip of his nose, making it easier for him to see his patients up close and look at the owners at the same time.

Walking out into the reception area, Doc was wiping his hands on a worn white towel, an indication that he had just completed an operation. Preoccupied with details pertaining to his last patient, he apologized before he even looked at his visitor.

"Sorry, my assistant's been under the weather the past couple of days. I told her to stay home and get better. Hope you haven't been waiting too long. What can I do for…?"

Doc stopped dead in his tracks as he got his first look at the person who'd walked into his clinic.

"Ramona?"

"You don't have an assistant, Doc," Mona reminded him with a smile. At least, he hadn't had one the last time she'd been by. He'd told her that she'd spoiled him for anyone else and he wasn't even going to attempt to replace her.

She'd rather liked that, even though she did acknowledge that it was a little vain on her part. "Do you?" she tagged on.

"Just Linda. She juggles my appointments," he explained, "but she doesn't like to be called a secretary. Says it's outdated. So I call her my assistant. It makes her happy." He tossed the towel aside on the reception desk and took hold of both of her hands in his wide, capable ones. "Here, let me look at you," he cried, as pleased as any father would be when his only daughter was finally home from college. "You look good," he declared. "But then, you always looked good," he amended.

And then he seemed contrite. "I'm sorry I missed your graduation, Ramona. I wanted to come, but Jake Sloan's mare was having trouble giving birth to her foal and I couldn't just leave her like that—"

"I know," she told him, cutting his unnecessary apology short. He wouldn't have been Doc if he'd left the mare in distress. And she wouldn't be where she was if he hadn't been that man. No way would she ever find fault with him. She dismissed the graduation ceremony with a few words. "It was just a couple of hours in a day. You were fighting to save the mare's life. Rick told me," she explained in response to the quizzical look the veterinarian gave her.

"Don't get me wrong, Doc," she continued quickly, in case he misunderstood. "I would have loved to have had you there, but I understand why you weren't. You're like a father to me. If it wasn't for you, I would have never been able to go to college, much less on to veterinary school. And you gave me my edge. I was ahead of the class because you allowed me to trail after you, letting me learn firsthand how to successfully treat sick animals. I'll never be able to even begin to pay you back for that."

He gestured to a seat beside the receptionist's desk and he sat down behind it. "You really want to pay me back?" he asked, studying her expression.

"You know I do."

"Then come join my practice."

Mona's mouth dropped open. This was what she'd been secretly hoping for all along, but they had never discussed her coming to work with him after she graduated. She'd thought that maybe he would have preferred working on his own.

She had to ask before she let herself begin celebrating. "Do you mean it?"

Doc chuckled. "Why do you think I sent you to veterinary college? I'm getting on in years, Ramona," he confided, leaning over the desk. "I'm not as young as I used to be—"

She cut him off. She didn't want him dwelling on age, didn't want to think about his ever getting old. She'd come to depend on the fact that he would always be there. Like Rick. It had been hard enough on her when her grandmother had died. There were times when she couldn't get herself to accept that. It felt too much like being abandoned.

"Sure you are, Doc," she told him with feeling. "You're the youngest man I know."

Doc grinned and it made him appear at least ten years younger. "Be that as it may, being the only vet in the area is really beginning to wear me down. I don't mind saying that I could use help. The right kind of help." He looked at her pointedly. "Your help. How about it? Are you game, Ramona?"

Unabashed enthusiasm throbbed in her voice as she told him, "Try and stop me."

Amused, pleased, he laughed at her challenge. "You're a force of nature, Ramona. I wouldn't dream of ever getting in your way."

Mona moved to the edge of the seat. "So when can I start?" she wanted to know.

He would have wanted her to begin yesterday. He really was swamped.

"I'd say 'now,' but realistically, how about right after your brother's wedding? I'm assuming that you want to pitch in with the preparations," he said knowingly. "From what I hear, Miss Joan's got the food covered, but there are still the decorations and all that stuff I have no idea about that needs doing. I'm sure that Olivia and Tina will appreciate the help."

Olivia and Tina. That would be her future sister-in-law and Olivia's sister. She'd met them both just once, at her graduation. Both were initially from Dallas and according to the brief explanation she'd gotten, Rick had met Olivia when she'd come looking for her runaway sister. Rick had brought them to her graduation, then dropped the little bombshell on her that he was getting married. *And* that Olivia was having his baby.

In all honesty, she was excited about the prospect of becoming an aunt, but not so much about becoming a sister-in-law. Or, more specifically, if she was being really honest with herself, she wasn't all that thrilled about Rick getting married. Though she would never tell him as much, she didn't want to lose him, or lose the connection they had. And wives had a way of doing that, cutting their man out from the herd and keeping him all to themselves.

For as long as she could remember, Rick had been part of her life. Even this morning's protective big-brother display was all part of the deal, even though she bristled and made noises that she was irritated and that he was cutting into her independence. But if Rick wasn't there to care about what she did, or who she did it with, she knew she would miss that terribly. Miss having him worrying about her.

Miss being the center of his world.

But now he was going to have a new center. Olivia was going to be his center. And she would be out in the cold.

Mona wasn't all that sure how she would handle that reality in the long run. That was what she needed to work out. But even as she thought about it, she could feel a loneliness seeping in.

"And," Doc was saying, "there's something else to consider."

She blinked. How much had she missed with her mind wandering? "What?"

"Well, it's no secret that Rick was hoping you'd open a practice in Dallas or Austin. There's a lot more money to be made in big cities like that. People have a lot more money to spend on their pets," he told her. "I know Rick's hoping that you'll become financially secure. That won't happen if you work with me."

Money had never been her primary concern. She wanted to stay in Forever, wanted to work with her mentor. "Don't worry about Rick. I doubt if he even remembers that he had any plans for my future," she said dismissively. "My brother's got more important things on his mind these days."

Doc watched her for a long moment. Something about his expression told her that he'd heard more than she'd been willing to say.

"Rick always struck me as a very capable young

man," Doc said. "I'm sure he can handle having a wife *and* a sister."

Was she that transparent, or was Doc just that good at reading people as well as animals?

Mona shrugged, doing her best not to look as if her brother's ability to be a husband and a brother mattered to her one way or the other.

"We'll see."

Just then the chimes in the doorway sounded, interrupting the flow of the conversation. Mona turned around in her seat, fully expecting to see another of Doc's patients being brought into the clinic.

Instead, Joe walked in.

"Thought you might be here," he said. And then, as an afterthought he nodded at the veterinarian, muttering Whitman's title by way of a greeting. "Doc."

"Why are you looking for me?" she asked. Suspicion crept into her voice. "Rick send you?"

"No, Rick left the office to see Olivia. Something about having to drive her to the next town for a doctor's appointment. I just thought you might want to know that Mick towed your car in and he's finished fixing your flat—and putting air into your spare," he added. "Car's waiting for you at his shop anytime you're ready to pick it up."

Mona nodded her thanks, then looked back at Doc. "Why would I want to go anywhere else?" she asked the older man. It was a rhetorical question. "Everyone takes such good care of me here. Besides, I do have that loan to pay back," she reminded him pointedly.

Doc waved his hand at her words, dismissing them.

"Wasn't a loan, it was a gift. A scholarship, if you will. You don't pay back a scholarship."

"Doc, you don't charge your patients much. You're hardly rolling in money. You can't afford to just give that kind of money away—even to me."

"Now, there you're wrong," Doc told her. "It's my money, which means that I'm at liberty to spend it any way I want. And what I wanted was to be part of creating the best damn veterinarian that this part of Texas has ever seen. You wouldn't begrudge an old man his dream, would you?"

"I already told you, I don't know any 'old man,' so there's no way I could begrudge him anything. As for you, I know that I owe you so much more than I can ever pay back. The money's the least of it."

"If it's the least of it, there's no point in even concerning yourself about it. Good, that's settled," Doc pronounced. "You're not paying me back."

Mona blinked, feeling a little dazed. Doc had somehow managed to twist her words. But this wasn't the end of the matter. She would find a way to get money into Doc's bank account without raising any red flags. Once it was there, he couldn't just hand it back to her. She wouldn't let him. His mentoring had been priceless and no way could she ever pay him back for sharing his time and himself with her.

But money was something she *could* return. And would.

"We'll see," she murmured.

Turning toward Joe, she asked, "Want to give me a ride over to Mick's Garage?"

"That's why I'm hanging around," the senior deputy told her.

That said, Joe turned on his heel and led the way out.

"See you later, Doc," Mona called out, following Joe.

"Later," Doc echoed. And smiled to himself.

Chapter Six

They looked good together.

Sitting at one of the tables set up for the reception, Mona felt a pang. She was watching her brother and his brand-new bride dancing together. Wearing a beautiful floor-length gown with an empire waist that softly swirled about her as she moved, Olivia looked radiant. The statuesque blonde had a double glow about her because she was not only a bride, but a mother-to-be, as well.

It was ordinarily not the best of combinations, but Mona had to admit that Olivia carried it off with aplomb. When she first met her sister-in-law last month, Mona was completely prepared to dislike the woman who was taking her brother away from her. But Olivia was smart, sharp and witty—and obviously very, very much in love with Rick.

It was the last quality that carried the most weight with Mona. If she had to lose Rick, lose the man who'd been brother, father *and* mother to her as far back as she could remember, she wanted it to be to a woman who had stars in her eyes every time she looked at him. That described Olivia to a *T.*

And Rick, well, Mona had to admit that she'd never seen him look so proud, so happy. Oh, he'd displayed both emotions at her recent graduation, but this, this was something different, something more. This demonstration of pride and happiness came from a man very obviously in love, who clearly felt that the sun rose and set around the woman he had just promised to love and cherish in sickness and in health until death reared its dark head to part them.

She knew that her brother had never thought true love was in the cards for him—honest-to-God, gut-twisting love. And now, here he was, dancing before the whole town and seeing only the woman in his arms.

Here he was, Mona thought, in love and a husband.

Not just a husband but a father-to-be, as well. He was taking on a great deal in a very short amount of time. And while she was glad for him, truly, truly glad because Rick deserved every bit of happiness that came his way, deep down she was still very sad for herself.

She'd done her very best not to show it, to throw herself wholeheartedly into festively decorating Doc's backyard—the veterinarian had generously thrown open his house because his was the largest backyard in the area and there were a lot of people who wanted to celebrate their sheriff's nuptials—so that no one would suspect that she struggled to keep this growing feeling of loneliness from consuming her.

It wasn't an unfamiliar feeling.

Mona had struggled with it before. This was the same loneliness that had come for her when their grandmother had died so suddenly when she was in

her second year at college. At the time, Rick had un-
knowingly made the loneliness retreat by promising
that she'd always have him to rely on, that he would
always be there for her, no matter what.

But today, his first priority had become his wife, as
it should be.

However, who did *she* have? Mona wondered, suppressing a sigh as she twirled the stem of her cham-
pagne glass, hardly aware of what she was doing.

Yes, technically, to the outside observer, her family
had just increased. She'd gained not only a sister-in-law,
but Olivia's sister, Tina, and nephew, Bobby, as well.
Yet that gain was just on paper. In her heart, she hadn't
gained, she'd lost. Lost a very, very important person
in her world.

She hated feeling like this, hated not being able to
simply celebrate Rick's happiness and just be *happy*
for him.

Rick and Olivia had each other and she…she had
Doc and the practice, Mona consoled herself. Doc had
no other family. *She* was going to have to be his family,
she reminded herself. And maybe, in time, that would
become enough. For her, as well.

Rick caught her eye as he twirled Olivia about on the
floor. He was grinning from ear to ear. Mona smiled
broadly for his benefit, silently telling herself to stop
being so maudlin. She loved Rick and she wanted him
to be happy.

Larry looked from his friend, to the sheriff's sister.
Mona was sitting several tables away from theirs. With
an annoyed sigh, Larry shook his head.

"So when are you going to make your move?" he finally asked Joe.

Preoccupied, Joe realized that the deputy beside him had addressed the question to him. Not that the question made any sense.

He blinked and stared at Larry. "What?"

Larry appeared ready to hit him upside the head. "Your move, man," he grounded out between clenched teeth. "When are you going to make your move?"

He was *not* going to encourage this. Turning away from Larry, Joe said, "I don't know what you're talking about."

Larry did not cease and desist, the way Joe had hoped. Instead, he asked another question, one that was just as annoying as the first.

"God, you're even thicker than a bale of hay, aren't you? You've been staring at Mona for the last half hour," Larry hissed. "If you stared any harder, your eyes would have fallen out of your head by now. She's alone, you're alone. *Do* something about it."

He was going to do something about it, Joe thought. He would go home in a few minutes, but not yet. Right now, he just wanted to look at Mona a few minutes longer. Dressed in a deep green cocktail dress that accentuated her small waist and clung invitingly to her curves, she was a vision he was sealing into his memory. A vision he couldn't get enough of.

"Maybe she wants to be alone," he pointed out to the blond deputy.

"Then she'd be smiling, wouldn't she?" Larry asked, gesturing toward Mona. "Is she smiling?"

Joe had a clear view of her profile. The corner of

her mouth was not curving and she wasn't given to lop-sided smiles. "No."

"I rest my case." Larry eyed him expectantly. When Joe gave no indication of moving from his seat, Larry shook his head and mumbled something about "hope-less." "You're going to die alone," the deputy said to him. "You know that, don't you?"

Frowning, Joe rose from the table. It wasn't clear whether he would take the advice he'd been given or if he just wanted to get away from the giver, but Larry went with the positive and nodded his approval.

"Good, now just put one foot in front of the other until you reach her table. When you do," Larry continued to coach, "you ask her to dance with you." Joe shot him a dark look. "The band's playing a slow dance. Everyone is capable of a slow dance. Even you," he insisted. "Just pretend to move your feet. The object is to have an excuse to take her into your arms and hold her."

But Joe remained in his spot. Larry's thin grasp on his temper snapped. "Damn it, Joe, if it all depended on you, there'd be no Apache nation." Larry scowled in frustration, but he was not about to give up. "Do I have to drag you over there?" he asked.

As close as Joe could figure, his friend had had three drinks at the reception so far and while that didn't make the tall deputy drunk or dangerous, Larry grew agitated.

Afraid that the man might do something that would wind up embarrassing him or worse, embarrassing Mona, Joe weighed the options and decided that it would be more prudent just to ask Mona to dance. If she turned him down, he could tell Larry to back off. If she took him up on it, well, so much the better.

Like Larry had said, he knew how to move his feet back and forth and sway in time to the music. Not much more was required in a slow dance. And it *did* give him the opportunity to hold Mona without any consequences.

"Stay put," Joe growled in a low voice. There was no missing the command in his tone. The last thing he wanted right now was a wing man, something he could see that Larry was more than ready to become.

Crossing from his table to Mona's, he searched his mind, looking for words that wouldn't instantly transform him into a fool.

Mona saved him the trouble.

Aware of the slight shadow that had fallen over her from behind, Mona turned in her seat and found herself looking up into Joe's ruggedly handsome face. If her heart leaped just a little, she told herself it was because he'd startled her.

"Hi," she murmured.

"Hi," he echoed.

So much for groundbreaking conversation.

Glancing over his own shoulder, he saw that Larry watched him intently and that the deputy was moving his hands in a gesture meant to urge him along. To get on with it already. Joe had a feeling that if he didn't progress any further, Larry would hurry to his side and take over like a frustrated puppeteer.

He turned back to Mona. "Feel like dancing?" he asked her.

No, what I feel like doing is sitting here, feeling sorry

for myself. But maybe dancing might help me get rid of that feeling, she thought.

"Sure," she answered. Her quick answer, she could see, surprised Joe. "Why not?"

Rising, she put her hand into his. Joe wrapped his fingers around it, turned on his heel and led her to the dance floor.

As he passed Larry, Joe deliberately refrained from making any eye contact with him. He sensed that the deputy probably congratulated himself on getting them together, as well as flashing some kind of sign meant to cheer him on. Larry had absolutely no handle on what was embarrassing behavior and what was acceptable.

They came to a stop on the edge of the dance floor. Mona turned her face up to his. "You sure your date won't mind you dancing with me?" she asked.

"I didn't bring a date—unless you count Larry." He looked down at her as if to probe her thoughts. "You're not counting Larry, are you?"

"No, I'm not counting Larry," she said with a wide grin. "You don't strike me as a couple."

She laughed and the light sound instantly burrowed under his skin, the way it always used to whenever he heard it. Though he wasn't prone to poetic thoughts by any stretch of the imagination, the sound of Mona's laughter always made him think of bluebells growing wild in the field. He wasn't sure as to why that was, but felt it was safer if he didn't explore his reaction.

The less he thought about Mona in general, the better. Except that since she'd returned two weeks ago, and especially since that first night in the cabin, he couldn't seem to make himself *stop* thinking about her.

Mona was one of the reasons he'd allowed himself to get roped into decorating the outside of Doc's place.

One? Hell, Mona was *the* reason he'd agreed to lend a hand. Sure, the sheriff was a man he not only admired but also liked and he wished Rick nothing but the very best with this marriage, but in general, outside of his job, Joe made it a rule to keep to himself whenever possible. Keeping to himself didn't include picking up a hammer and hanging up streamers or building a dance floor or the trellis where the happy twosome and one quarter—if you counted the baby—exchanged their marriage vows.

But the sheriff was Mona's brother and pitching in with the decorating allowed him to be around her. He'd assumed, rightly so, that she would be in the thick of it, at least working if not actually ordering people around, telling them what to do and, more likely than not, how to do it.

"Something wrong?" he asked her as he threaded one hand through hers while lightly placing the other around her waist. He tried not to think how good she felt in his arms.

And how much he wanted to kiss her again.

Mona gazed up at him, cocking her head as if she was trying to understand. "No. Why? Do I look like there's something wrong?"

"Well…" Backtracking, he reconsidered his assessment. "You don't exactly look like there's something right."

She pretended to shake her head as if she was trying to clear it. "Is this something new? I don't remember you talking in riddles."

"I don't remember you sidestepping and being evasive," he countered. He told himself to remember to sway to the music. The natural rhythm within his body took over. "C'mon, Mona, this is me. You used to be able to tell me what was bothering you," he reminded her.

"I also used to be able to skim rocks along the surface of the lake," she answered flippantly. "I can't do that anymore."

He stared at her for a moment. The sun was still in the sky, allowing him to look into her eyes, to see the things that she wasn't saying. "When was the last time you tried?"

Shrugging, Mona deliberately looked away. "I don't remember."

Just as he thought. "Then how do you know you *can't* still skim rocks on the lake?" he challenged. He saw the exasperation that entered her eyes as she turned back and raised her chin. He knew that stance. She was on the brink of picking a fight. "Tell you what, after your brother and his wife make a break for it to go on their honeymoon, why don't you and I go down to the lake and test that theory of yours?"

She shook her head, rejecting the suggestion. "It's not that important."

He surprised Mona by agreeing with her. "No, but maybe if you find out that you can still skim rocks over the lake, you'll think of me as your friend again and tell me what's bothering you."

He was making sense. She had no use for sense right now and just wanted to be agreed with and left alone.

"Shut up and dance," she ordered in barely suppressed exasperation.

"There's that winning personality of yours again," he declared with a grin. If looks could kill, he'd be lying on the floor, dead on the spot, he thought. He feigned ducking her glare. "I'm dancing, I'm dancing," he told her.

The silence between them lasted less than thirty seconds. The look she flashed him when she leaned back was apologetic. "I'm being prickly again, aren't I?"

"Yeah, but your brother just got married, so I'm cutting you a little slack."

Mona eyed him sharply. "Get out of my head, Joe."

A so-called contrite expression on his face, he danced her in a semicircle. "Yes, ma'am."

Mona closed her eyes. "Oh, God, I'm not a 'ma'am,' Joe. Don't call me that," she told him sharply. "It makes me feel totally ancient."

"Every female above the age of ten in this part of the country is politely addressed as 'ma'am.' You know that. You also know that you're not ancient," he pointed out. The song came to an end and, reluctantly, Joe released her. Or at least he dropped his hands. But his eyes held her in place far more effectively than his hands could ever do. "You want to go somewhere and talk?"

The suggestion did not meet with her approval. She knew that if she went with him, she'd say far too much, and right now she didn't like herself, didn't like how she was feeling. It didn't point to the person she really was. What it did was make her out to be a spoiled, self-centered child and it was bad enough that she knew that. She didn't need anyone else aware of the fact.

"No," she answered much too quickly, then shrugged as she looked away. She tossed him a bone, hoping it would get him to back away. "Maybe later."

"How much later?" he pressed. "A couple of hours? A couple of days? A couple of decades?"

She sighed. "Just later."

By then she hoped to have worked out what was bothering her. Hoped to finally react maturely, the way she knew in her heart she should.

The way she knew that right now, she wasn't.

That was what bothered her. That she should be putting Rick first, the way he'd always done with her. She should just be happy for him with his new life.

But all she could think was that their paths had suddenly diverged and he was going off in another direction. A direction she would never be able to follow. Not even with his example leading the way. Because in her heart, she knew she would never trust anyone else, never give them her heart the way Rick had given his to Olivia.

Mona knew, as surely as she was standing here on this temporary dance floor, that someday, the person she gave her heart to—if she was ever so foolish—would desert her. Would leave her behind as surely as her father had, as surely as her grandmother had.

As her mother had.

Except for Rick, none of the important people in her life had remained. Granted she'd never known her father and both he and her grandmother had died, but the bottom line was that they were gone.

As gone as her mother was. Her mother who had left both Rick and her with Abuela, promising to be back "soon." And "soon," it seemed, had no end, no finite definition.

At least not to Elena Santiago.

"Okay," Joe was saying to her gamely. "You got it. Later it is."

She sighed. "You're like some kind of a pit bull, aren't you? Latching on and refusing to let go."

If she thought she was insulting him, she miscalculated. He grinned at her instead. "You don't know the half of it."

"And I don't think I want to know," she told him. She saw a strange, alert look come into his eyes as he glanced past her. "Okay, now what?" she asked.

Instead of Joe answering, she heard a woman behind her say, "Hello, Ramona."

Curious, not recognizing the voice, Mona turned around. And found herself looking up into a face that was familiar to her even though she couldn't really place it.

A face that looked like an older version of hers.

"Hello," she replied guardedly. No name came to her as she appraised the dark-haired, dark-eyed woman. "I'm sorry. Do I know you?"

"No, not really," the woman answered. "But I'm hoping to change that." Before Mona could ask how she intended to do that or why she wanted to, the woman said, "I'm your mother, Ramona," and promptly generated an earthquake in her world.

Chapter Seven

Joe knew that Mona hated having anyone butt in to her business. She took it as an insinuation that she was incapable of handling her own affairs, of dealing with whatever curve nature happened to throw at her. A smart man would have just kept to the shadows and let things play out without interfering.

Maybe, when it came to things that concerned Mona, he just wasn't smart.

Because, despite all he knew to the contrary, he could feel that same protective instinct that had kicked in the evening of the flash floods.

Mona had visibly stiffened when the woman said she was her mother. He knew this would not turn into a happy reunion complete with tears of joy. Mona had told him a long time ago that she wanted nothing to do with the woman who had been able to walk away from her and her brother without so much as a single qualm.

He also knew that Elena Santiago had come back to Forever once before. She'd shown up on Rick's doorstep eighteen years after she'd disappeared out of her children's lives. The way he'd heard the story, Elena had wanted to make amends, but Rick would have none of it. He had deliberately sent her away before Mona came home from school. He hadn't wanted his sister to be upset by the reappearance of a mother who didn't know the meaning of the title.

As far as Joe knew, Mona never met her mother that day. Judging from the way she'd blankly stared at the woman before Elena had told her who she was, he was right. Mona had no idea what her mother looked like.

Until now.

Taking his cue from Mona's stiff posture, Joe moved forward, ever so slightly placing himself between her and the woman claiming to be her mother.

In her day, Elena had been a very beautiful woman who turned the heads of men and women alike as she passed. Even now, she was still a very attractive woman and it was obvious that she was accustomed to getting by on her looks and using those looks.

After giving him a flirtatious smile, making no secret of the fact that she took full measure of him, Elena turned to Mona. "Is this your man?"

Mona's eyes narrowed into angry slits. "You don't have the right to ask me anything or know anything about me."

It was obvious that Elena didn't think her daughter meant what she said. With a tolerant smile, she tried again. "Ramona—"

Mona was not about to be won over. Her brother and his wife had gone to change into their traveling clothes. She wanted this woman gone before they returned. "You gave up that right a long time ago. Now, please leave before Rick sees you."

"Protective," Elena said with a nod. "Like your brother. Your brother's wedding is why I came back."

"Why?" Mona demanded, struggling to keep her voice down. For her brother's sake, she wanted no undue attention drawn to this woman. "So you can ruin that, too?"

Elena appeared a little hurt by her daughter's accusation. Joe noted that she rallied, keeping her smile in place.

"No," Elena told her. "So I could make amends. A wedding is a celebration of a new beginning. I thought Enrique might want to make that new beginning knowing he had a mother in the background who wanted—"

Mona cut her off. She didn't want to listen to theatrical rhetoric.

"Don't you understand? You have no right to want anything," she informed the other woman coldly. "Now, I'm asking you nicely, please leave. If you care anything at all about Rick the way you claim, you'll go without causing a scene. Rick doesn't need to know that you're here."

Joe could see that the woman struggled between her own desire to put the sins of her past behind her and doing as her daughter requested.

In the end, Joe took over. He politely but firmly took hold of Mona's mother by the arm and escorted her out of the backyard.

"This way, please, Mrs. Santiago," he said, gesturing toward the front of the two-story house.

Elena gave him no opposition, allowing herself to be led away.

"Ruiz," she corrected him, regally walking toward the front of the house as if all eyes were on her. "It's Mrs. Ruiz now."

"You got married again?" Joe asked, not because he was curious but because he saw that the woman wanted him to ask. It cost him nothing to play along.

Elena nodded. "Twice." She leaned her head in toward him and lowered her voice as if she was sharing something in confidence. "Men keep dying on me," she said with a deep sigh. "I seem to have the worst luck."

"Not as bad as the men," Joe commented without a hint of humor.

Elena laughed anyway. In contrast to her daughter, Elena's laugh was deep and throaty, as if she had spent a good deal of the past eighteen years sipping whiskey at the elbows of fawning men.

But something about the way she cocked her head and her stance, that reminded him of Mona. Like it or not, the two women were connected.

Elena pressed her lips together, clearly debating asking him a question. She decided to put it to him. "Think that Ramona will ever forgive me?" she asked without preamble.

He considered the question in light of what he remembered about Mona's character when they were much younger.

"She's stubborn, but she's got a good heart. But getting Mona to come around won't come easy," he warned the other woman.

Elena barely suppressed a sigh and nodded. "I

didn't think it would, but I knew I had to take that first step."

In her eyes, Joe saw a sadness that transcended the bravado she presented to the world.

"Be good to Ramona and protect her," she instructed him.

Joe could just see the way Mona would react if she overheard her mother telling him that. "That's not my call," he answered.

Elena watched him for a long moment and he could almost feel her eyes burrowing into him.

"Oh, but I think it is," Elena contradicted. She slipped her hand into his and then shook it. "Tell her I'll be seeing her again." She flashed a broad, telling smile. "And maybe next time, we can work things out."

I wouldn't hold my breath if I were you, Mrs. Ruiz, Joe thought. But he kept his opinion to himself. No sense in getting the woman upset.

She squeezed his hand, as if they had made some sort of a pact, and then walked away, making her way to her black sedan.

He didn't waste any more time watching her. The noise from behind the house picked up and that could only mean one thing. Rick and Olivia were about to leave on their honeymoon. He didn't want to miss saying goodbye to the couple.

Or being there for Mona when they finally left. He had a feeling she'd need him.

Joe made it around to the back just in time. Rick and Olivia had all but come to the end of the line of people who wanted to wish them well.

Rick glanced his way as he approached and grinned,

looking somewhat relieved. "Thought maybe you decided to back out on me," Rick said.

Joe thought it was an odd choice of words. But the sheriff's flippant tone told him that Rick *hadn't* noticed his mother crashing the party, which, all things considered, was a good thing. He was careful, though, not to look relieved. He didn't want to trigger any questions. It wasn't in his nature to lie outright.

Instead, he picked up the thread of what Rick had just said. "Back out?" he echoed.

"Yeah. I'm leaving the office—and the post—in your hands." Rick seemed pleased with the decision he made earlier while making arrangements to book his honeymoon. "You're going to be the sheriff of Forever for the next three weeks."

Joe looked at the bridegroom, stunned. "Sheriff?" he repeated numbly.

Rick laughed at the completely stoic expression. "Yeah. Sheriff. What's the matter?" he asked. "You forget you're the senior deputy?"

He hadn't forgotten, he just never thought it put him at the head of the line for anything. He wasn't the competitive type. "No, but I just thought that Larry—or maybe Alma—would be your first choice to fill the position."

But Rick shook his head. "Larry and Alma are good people, but you're the head deputy and it's about time you tried out your wings to see if you can fly, Joe."

"Flying" held no appeal to him. He liked being under the radar. Liked just doing his job, taking care of what he was responsible for and not worrying about any big pictures that might be lying around, needing to be considered.

"Maybe I don't want to fly," he told Rick. "Maybe I just want to walk to wherever it is that I'm supposed to be going."

"Sorry." Rick clapped him heartily on the back. "Decision's been made. Right now, you've gotta fly." He gave his senior deputy an encouraging look. "I'll see you when I get back."

"*We'll* see you when we get back," Olivia corrected, slipping her arm through his and smiling up at her husband's face with the eyes of a woman who was head over heels in love.

"Right. *We'll* see you when I—when *we*—get back," he amended with a quick grin to Olivia. "This 'couple' business is going to take a while for me to get the hang of," he confided more to Olivia than to the reluctant deputy standing before him.

"You'll get used to it," Doc assured him with a hearty laugh. The veterinarian had come up behind Joe as Rick was telling the deputy that he had been temporarily promoted. Doc curled his fingers about the letter-sized envelope he was holding. "Of course, I wouldn't know about that from firsthand experience, but that's what people tell me."

"Yeah, that's what I hear, too," Rick told him, looking at his bride with a boundless affection. And then he turned toward Joe again. "In the meantime, I want you to look after Mona for me."

That made two people who were entrusting him with Mona's care in a short amount of time. Mona would have been fit to be tied if she knew.

"I'll try," Joe promised honestly. "But it won't be easy." Rick looked at him quizzically. "She doesn't like anyone hovering over her," Joe pointed out.

"Then don't let her see you hovering," said Rick. He looked around the immediate vicinity and frowned slightly. "Speaking of my sister, where is she? I kind of thought I'd see her before we left."

"Maybe she doesn't like saying goodbye," Joe suggested.

The two men looked at one another, as if communicating in silence what they couldn't in words.

Mona had never been much for goodbyes.

"Yeah, maybe," Rick agreed vaguely.

Doc moved forward, taking both of Olivia's hands in his and managing to secretly slip the envelope he'd been holding into them. It was a little something to help out with expenses when they got to their Southern California destination, a charming little bed-and-breakfast just north of San Diego.

"You two have a safe flight. Now *go*," Doc ordered, releasing Olivia's hands and taking a step backward away from the couple. "Before someone decides they just have to talk to you before you leave."

"Good advice," Rick agreed.

He took Olivia's hand in his and together they made a run for it through the house and out front to his Jeep. The vehicle stood waiting for them, already gaudily decorated to announce to the world at large that they had gotten married today.

A crowd of well-wishers were at their backs, pelting them not with rice but with choruses of good wishes and orders to enjoy themselves and not to come back too fast. Forever, like the town's name promised, would be here waiting for them.

Turning away from the speeding vehicle as it disappeared down the road, Joe scanned the faces that had poured out of the backyard with him.

Mona wasn't among them.

As he looked second time, his eyes met Larry's. Joe made his way over to the other deputy to enlist his help.

"You seen Mona around?" he asked Larry, trying his best to keep the impatience gnawing away at him out of his voice.

Larry didn't even have to pretend to think. "You mean, just a few minutes ago? Yeah, she was heading your way." He pointed to the encroaching darkness, indicating the infinite vastness that stood at the back of Doc's property. "I thought that maybe you were taking my advice and the two of you were rendezvousing." Larry drew out every one of the four syllables, making the word sound as if it had twice as many letters in it as it did. "Guess I thought wrong." But he found himself talking to Joe's back. Joe headed toward the rear of the yard, a purpose to his gait. "You know where she is?" Larry called after his friend.

"I've got a hunch," Joe tossed over his shoulder, moving quickly. In a few seconds, he was out of earshot.

Twilight crept in and, as it approached, systematically erased any decent visibility. If he didn't find her soon, he might not be able to until the next morning. The city proper had streetlights, but if Mona had gone where he thought she might have, there weren't any streetlights to illuminate the way for her.

Or him.

He had a flashlight in the glove compartment of his vehicle, but he hadn't thought to get it and he was already too far out on the road to the woods to double back for it now.

He moved quickly, the way he'd learned as a boy. Back then he'd had to jump aside to get of the way of his uncle's long, powerful reach as the latter swung his fisted hand at him. The man had only done that when he got drunk, but he'd been drunk pretty much most of the time.

And eventually, alcohol did the six-foot-five man in, and indirectly, alcohol had taken his mother, as well. She was run over by a drunk driver who didn't even realize that he had hit her.

As for him, Joe took what he could from every life experience and his uncle's drunken temper had taught him how to move fast, how to *be* fast. And while his tolerance for the substance for some reason was unusually high, he never tried to uncover his limits. He didn't want to know. But his uncle's substance abuse had at least enabled him to become a fast runner.

Most nights Joe would be down the road, running for the shelter of the woods behind his house before his uncle even rose to his wobbly feet.

Joe ran now, ran toward the lake where he'd guessed Mona would be, since they'd talked about it earlier.

And he'd guessed right, he saw, as the lake came into view.

The full moon was seductively bouncing its beams

off the water. Competing, it seemed, with Mona who was skimming flat, smooth stones along the lake's surface.

Joe stopped running and slowed down to a walk. A languid one. He didn't want to startle her.

And he did like looking at Mona when she thought that she was alone. Some of the tension in her face and body had faded and she became more like the girl he'd once known.

The girl he'd once thought about in the wee hours of the night.

He'd been right, Joe thought as he continued observing Mona. She hadn't lost her touch. The stones that left her fingers skimmed along the surface of the lake as if it was solid, made out of spun glass rather than liquid.

She didn't seem to notice. The look on her face was one of preoccupation. He guessed that it had little to do with skimming stones along a lake and everything to do with the woman who had returned, uninvited, into her life.

Chapter Eight

Several minutes slipped away as Joe continued to stand there, watching her as she skimmed stones. If Mona turned around now and saw him, she might think he was stalking her.

So he resumed walking, and as he came up to her, he announced his presence by saying, "Told you that you hadn't lost your touch."

Lost in conflicting thoughts that assaulted her from all directions, Mona jumped at the sound of Joe's voice. She spun around, ready to pelt whomever with the stones in her hand. She let loose with two, aiming them at the source of the voice like a modern-day David firing rocks at Goliath. All that was missing was the slingshot.

Joe instinctively ducked and dodged to the left as one smooth black stone flew by his head, missing contact by less than an inch.

"Hey, whoa!" he protested, holding his hands up in semisurrender. "I come in peace."

Recognition sank in. Swallowing an oath, Mona dropped the last three stones, the sound of contact with the ground muffled by the grass.

Realizing that she could have seriously hurt him had he not moved, fear instantly morphed into anger. "Damn it, Joe, you should know better than to sneak up behind a person."

"I wasn't sneaking," he pointed out, joining her. "I was talking."

She dusted off her hands. Joe couldn't have been more than a few feet away when he spoke, which meant that he had to have soundlessly crossed over several yards to reach her.

"You didn't make any noise when you came up behind me," she accused. In her book, that qualified as "sneaking."

"I'm not supposed to," he answered glibly. "Moving around without making any noise is incorporated into my genes, remember?"

Mona frowned, grateful that she hadn't really hurt him. "I don't care about your genes, wear noisier boots," she ordered.

He liked the way the full moon scattered its light along her hair. She wore it loose and long. It flowed passed her shoulders like black steam.

Joe roused himself, focusing on the conversation. "I'll look into that as soon as your brother comes back from his honeymoon." Mona glared at him as if she didn't follow. "I'm not going to have time for anything else right now. He made me temporary acting sheriff."

"Good for you," she said with more enthusiasm than he thought she would feel, hearing the news. He hadn't thought that she cared what he did, as long as he stayed on the right side of the law, a fact that had been in some doubt in his earlier years.

Right now, she seemed more pleased with this temporary appointment than he was. "Yeah, well, we'll see," he said with a careless shrug.

He was definitely not comfortable with his new role, but he hadn't thought it right to mount an argument with a new husband driving off on his honeymoon. He doubted if Rick would have heard a word he said in his own defense.

Joe took in the surroundings. Listening, he could hear the stealth movement of several creatures that called the immediate area home. Looking at Mona, he doubted that she could run very fast in that tight dress should the occasion arise.

"You shouldn't be out here alone like this," he said.

"I know everyone in town," she argued. Nobody would try to hurt her, or take advantage of the situation. Besides, Rick had taught her enough defensive moves when she was younger.

"Not the drifters," he told her. "Forever gets its share."

She knew that there were women—probably more than a few—who liked the idea of a big, strong man protecting them. But she didn't number herself as being one of them. If you depended on no one, then you weren't disappointed when they didn't come through.

"I wasn't aware that there was a databank somewhere, distributing drifters. What *is* our share?" she asked flippantly. "One and a half a year? Maybe two?"

He wasn't about to let himself get sucked into a mindless argument for no reason. Besides, he knew she picked fights when she was upset. Not that he could blame her for feeling the latter. Having her mother appear out of nowhere was tantamount to a sucker punch.

"How are you?" he asked quietly.

As they started to walk back to Doc's, she plucked a wildflower growing in the grass and began to pull off its petals one by one. No singsong rhyme involving love accompanied their individual descent. Just nervous energy.

"I'm coming to terms with it," she answered with a sigh. "Things can't stay frozen forever, I know that. And if I decide to move to Dallas or Austin the way Rick wants me to, I'll feel better about leaving him if I know he has someone to watch over him. I guess that it's just going to take me a bit longer to ad—"

Joe interrupted her before she got any further. "I'm not talking about Rick getting married."

"Oh?" Mona responded innocently, avoiding his eyes. "What are you talking about?"

Her voice always got a little higher when she was lying. "You know what I'm talking about. Don't play dumb, Mona. You're smarter than that."

She resumed walking again, still avoiding his eyes. But there was no point pretending.

"I don't know about that," she said. "If I were smarter, then I wouldn't let it bother me at all."

He knew what she was saying, that she would be devoid of any emotions. He'd been that route himself. Hell, most of the time, he still opted for that route. But that wasn't Mona's way. "Then you'd be a brick wall," he told her.

Maybe that was for the best. "I can handle that." The wildflower had been plucked clean. She let the stem fall from her fingers. "Brick walls don't hurt."

Everyone hurt sometime, even if they didn't let on, Joe thought. "Unless someone takes a wrecking ball to them."

"They still don't hurt," she insisted. "They just crumble, but they don't hurt."

"Do you?" He placed his hand on her shoulder, stopping her from taking another step. Very gently, he turned her around to face him. "Hurt?" he added when she said nothing.

Mona shrugged off his hand and continued walking. He noticed that she'd raised her chin stubbornly. Another typical move for her. "Why do you care if I do or not?"

"Because I'm your friend, Mona. That's what friends do, they care. Even when they want to strangle their friends, they care," he told her evenly.

His answer coaxed a half smile out of her. It was his first indication that he had reached her.

"That's better," he said.

She let out a long breath and slowed her pace to match her cadence.

"Not really," she responded. "Why did she have to turn up like this? And now, of all times. What does she want, Joe?"

Maybe he was wrong, but he didn't believe there was an ulterior motive involved. "I think she—" he carefully avoided using the label *mother* "—wants what she said. To make up. To show you she's sorry."

Mona closed her eyes for a second, shaking her head. "It's too late for that."

He thought like that once, thought his life was set on a course to eventual destruction. And then a friend of his uncle pointed out that he was the master of his own destiny—and that nothing was written in stone. That had been his turning point.

Looking back, it probably saved him from a premature death.

"It's only too late if one of you is dead," he told her firmly.

"Well, then it's too late," she answered with finality. "Because she's dead to me. And if you're my friend the way you claim, you'll stop talking about it. Talk about something else."

"Okay." Joe looked up at the stars, thinking. And then he asked, "Think the Dallas Cowboys have a shot at the Super Bowl this year?"

She laughed and felt some of the tension drain away. "You don't like sports."

"No," he agreed. "But I was looking for a topic that wouldn't make you want to bite my head off."

She felt a flash of embarrassment. "I'm sorry, Joe. I'm a little edgy, I guess. This whole wedding thing was really unexpected and then *she* blows in from nowhere. I guess I got a little out of sorts."

He looked at her. "Mount St. Helens was a little out of sorts when it erupted. This is something a whole lot bigger."

She's stopped walking again. Wrapping her arms

around herself, she looked up at the sky. The darkness peaceful.

"Show me the Big Dipper, Joe," she asked, glancing toward him. "I always have trouble visualizing it when you're not there to point it out to me."

"There never seem to be as many stars in the big city as there are out here," he told her. "Maybe they just don't like all the noise."

She laughed and realized that she felt a lot better. Joe's always had a way of making her feel better.

"That has to be it," she agreed, tongue in cheek.

He moved directly behind her, to get the same perspective as she had. The breeze shifted just then and the scent of her hair seemed to fill his senses, making him dizzy. But he didn't step back. Instead, he pointed to a group of stars, drawing imaginary lines between them with his index finger.

"It's right there," he told her.

She saw it then. Joe always made it seem so easy. "Oh, you're right," she cried, turning her head toward him as she spoke.

Mona was acutely aware that she had brushed against him, not just with her hair, but with parts of her body, as well. Parts that felt as if they were shooting static electricity pulses all through her.

She drew in her breath slowly and then took a tentative step back. If she didn't, she would do something stupid. Like kiss him again. This time, there was no half-filled bottle of aged whiskey to blame it on.

He could feel the tension. Feel the attraction. He did his best to block both and didn't quite succeed.

"Want me to take you home?" Joe heard himself asking.

Home.

It would seem really empty tonight, she thought sadly. Without Rick, without her grandmother, it was just an old building with old memories. Rick wouldn't return for twenty-one days. And once he did get back, her brother would be sharing the house with Olivia. And, very soon, with their baby.

There wasn't a place for her in this house. Never mind that there was a third bedroom. She would still be the fifth wheel.

The thought pressed down heavily on her.

Mona pushed it aside, unable to deal with it just now.

She'd come to the wedding with Rick, but he had taken his car in order to drive himself and Olivia to the airport several towns away. That meant that she would either need a ride or have to walk home. Joe, she was certain, would lecture her if she chose the latter. It was simpler to accept the offer for a ride.

"Sure," she answered. "Might as well go home while it still is home."

Joe wasn't sure he understood her meaning. "You want to explain that?"

Did he need a road map? "Well, when they come back from their honeymoon, Rick and Olivia are going to be living there." Doc's house was coming into view in the horizon. She hoped that most of the people at the reception had already gone home. She didn't feel like talking to anyone. Except for maybe Joe. He somehow seemed to lure the words right out of her.

"Last I heard, three's a crowd unless one of the three is a product of the other two, like the baby," she continued. "I'm going to need a place to stay." Her mouth curved. "Maybe I can buy and fix up the old Murphy place."

To her surprise, Joe didn't laugh that off the way she'd expected him to. Instead, he managed to throw her completely by saying, "Well, that's something to think about."

The cabin smelled of the past and creatures that had crawled in there to die. She couldn't see herself staying in the Murphy place, except in an emergency, the way she had that first night when the storm hit. "I was just kidding, Joe."

"I'm not," he replied matter-of-factly. "It's not as if there's a handy apartment building in town. Or even a hotel where you can stay indefinitely. Taking that into consideration, I'm sure Rick and Olivia won't mind having you around—"

There was no way she was going to impose on her brother and his wife unless both her legs were broken. Which they weren't. "Right. A couple just back from their honeymoon really *love* having an extra person hovering around."

Ordinarily, she would have considered moving in with Miss Joan, who had room to spare. But that was no longer an option. "Tina and Bobby have already moved in with Miss Joan," she murmured, voicing her thoughts.

The owner of the diner had taken a real shine to Tina's baby and enjoyed having her quiet home finally filled with the sound of voices. In exchange, Olivia's younger sister was taking care of the house for the older woman, gladly doing all the things that Miss Joan found exceptionally tedious.

"You could move in with me," Joe suggested, catching her completely off guard with his suggestion.

Mona started, then regained her composure. "Yeah, that'll go over really well." And then she smiled, amused. "It'll certainly give the town something new to gossip about."

Gossip had never bothered him. No matter where he was, he'd always thought of himself as an outsider. Living in Forever and working as a deputy was the closest he'd ever come to being part of something.

"Doesn't bother me if it doesn't bother you," he told her.

She stopped walking and looked at him for a long moment. Was Joe saying what she thought he was saying—or was he completely oblivious to the way his offer could be interpreted?

"If you're still living where you were when I went away to school, you've only got one bedroom," she said pointedly.

She wasn't exactly telling him something new. "I am and I know. You take the bed, I'll take the sofa—like in the cabin," he added, humor entering his voice, as well as his eyes. "Anyway, it's just until we get the Murphy cabin fixed up." There was also another possibility, he reminded himself. "Or you decide to move away."

She didn't hear the last sentence, or the forced nonchalance that he'd woven through it. "You're serious about the cabin, aren't you?" she asked.

The more he thought about it, the better the solution

seemed. "Why not? The foundation's solid. We can go to the county office and find out who owns the property and make a bid for it."

There was one little thing wrong with his reasoning now that she gave it some serious thought. "I'm not exactly flush at the moment. I've got about two hundred dollars to my name," she calculated, then amended, "Maybe less."

"That's okay. I've got more."

For as long as she'd known him, Joe had never had much. In high school he'd worked odd jobs on weekends in order to pay for things like clothes and whatever else he needed. He never had any extra money to throw around, the way a few of the more privileged kids did.

"How much more?" she asked now, curious.

"More," he repeated. When she looked at him quizzically, he said, "I've got simple needs. Don't need much," he emphasized, "so I've been banking the rest." He spared her a glance, allowing himself a smile. "Waiting for a rainy day."

"And I qualify as a rainy day?" she guessed.

"You qualify as a whole storm on the horizon," he corrected her. They were almost at Doc's property, so Joe tabled the discussion. "We'll talk about this on Monday," he promised. "Right now, let's just get you home."

That was when she remembered.

"Can't just yet." Joe looked at her, waiting for an explanation. "I just remembered that I volunteered for the cleanup committee." She felt she had to, since she was, after all, the groom's sister.

"I can wait," he told her.

Knowing that Joe would be taking her home made her feel a great deal better without her really under-standing why. Right now, it was just too much to deal with, she told herself, mentally shoving all of it to the side for the time being.

She grinned at Joe. "You can do better than that. You can help me with the cleanup."

When she had gotten him to "help set up" he'd found himself pulled into a frenzy of work that had only ended in the early hours of this morning. This had the makings of the same thing. He didn't want her to think that he could be won over so easily. It might make her guess how he really felt about her.

"Do I have a choice in this?" Joe wanted to know.

Mona gave him a look that clearly said, "Not really," even though out loud she said, "Yes."

"But if I make the wrong choice, you won't be happy about it," he wisely guessed.

The smile on her lips had made its way to her eyes. He remembered how much he liked to see her that way. If he wasn't careful, he could lose himself in her eyes.

"Something like that," Mona answered.

"You know," Joe said with a reminiscent note in his voice as he entered Doc's side yard directly behind her. "I forgot how peaceful things were without having you around."

She sniffed. "The word is *boring*."

Joe inclined his head and said in a voice that was devoid of emotion, "If you say so."

Miss Joan was still there at the diner, overseeing her

waitresses who bussed the tables and stacked dishes in Doc's kitchen. Some of the men were taking down the different-sized tables that had been donated from various households, giving the reception a very unique look.

Still another group, co-ed this time, took down the gaily colored crepe lanterns and other decorations that had been made just for the occasion.

A wave of nostalgia hit Mona as she looked around. All of this struck her as a beehive of activity. There was nothing like this to be found in the big city, she thought with a touch of pride. People were just not that invested in their neighbors.

"Hey, Doc," Miss Joan called out, crossing back to the yard. The large man currently supervised the dismantling of the trellis used in the wedding. As he turned in her direction, graying tufts of unruly eyebrows raised silently in response to his name. "Where do you keep your dishwasher?" Miss Joan asked.

The veterinarian held up his wide, hamlike hands and wiggled them in the air. "At the ends of my wrists," he told her.

The girl who had come out with Miss Joan groaned. "No dishwasher?"

"It's all in how you look at it." Doc Whitman chuckled.

"I'll do them," Mona volunteered.

Miss Joan eyed at her skeptically. "Careful what you raise your hand for, honey. You know how many dishes there are?" the woman asked.

Mona grinned. "I was at the reception, remember?

The place was packed. Everyone had at least one dish if not two or three. I know what I'm up against."

"You're going to be washing dishes into the middle of next Tuesday," Miss Joan warned.

"Not if she has help," Joe muttered under his breath. He pretty much knew what was coming. If he had to pitch in, then he might as well be doing it on a joint project with Mona.

"Nice of you to volunteer," Miss Joan declared with a vigorous nod of her head. After stripping off her apron, she held it out to Joe.

Try as she might, Mona couldn't picture Joe doing something so utterly domestic. "You don't have to do this," Mona told him.

He shrugged. "Gotta do something, waiting to take you home."

"You could come back," she suggested, feeling guilty for having roped him in. "Or I could get a ride from someone else."

"Shut up and wash," he instructed, nodding toward the house.

"Yes, Joe," she answered meekly as she walked into the kitchen.

He wasn't buying her meek act for a second, Joe thought, following her inside. But he really did like the way it sounded.

Chapter Nine

The two-story house looked unusually dark to Mona as she and Joe drove toward it. As if the life, the heart, had been siphoned out, leaving the shell.

That morning, as she and Rick had driven away from the house on their way to Doc's and the wedding, the sun had been bright overhead and the air had been pregnant with the promise of a new beginning. Rick had been so nervous that she'd volunteered to drive.

She was happy for him while sad for herself. But the main thing was that Rick deserved to be happy. He'd always put her and their grandmother first, becoming the man of the house way before a male should have to even consider taking on the role.

In all the excitement and rush this morning, she hadn't thought to leave a light on for tonight when she returned alone. Hadn't thought about how dark and gloomy it would seem to come back to a house where there was no one to respond to the sound of her voice.

She thought about it now.

Joe drove his Jeep up to front of the old house. Stopping, he pulled up the hand brake, put the vehicle into

Park and turned off the ignition. Only then did he look in Mona's direction. He sensed rather than saw the tension roaming through her.

"We're here," he said when she made no move to get out.

She glanced at him. "You really didn't have to tell me that. I do recognize the house."

Mona took a deep breath, not wanting to go inside just yet. Once she shut the door behind her, that was it. She would be alone with her thoughts and right now, especially with her mother's sudden reappearance, she really didn't want to have time to think. Tired, she still felt way too wound up to fall asleep.

The night loomed before her like an unfriendly stranger.

She supposed that she could find something to do to keep busy until she felt ready to go to bed. There were still boxes that she'd shipped from Dallas when she'd relocated. This would be a good time to unpack them.

Settling in at Doc's Animal Clinic had gone far better. She'd already shelved all her references books and brought in a few things to personalize her space. But when it came to this house where she'd been raised, she had only unpacked the bare necessities.

Subconsciously, she supposed that pointed to her feeling that she was just a temporary guest and that she needed to be ready to leave at a moment's notice.

She was lost in thought, not reaching for the door handle. Joe interpreted it the only way he could. Mona didn't want to be alone tonight. "You want me to go in with you?"

Joe's low voice cut into her thoughts, bringing her back to the Jeep and the fact that she was still sitting in it. Shaking free of the mood that had all but wrapped itself around her, she looked at Joe, doing her best to appear bright-eyed and alert. But she still didn't know what he'd just said to her.

"What?"

"Inside." Joe nodded toward the house. "Do you want me to go into the house with you?" he asked pointedly.

There was no pity in his voice, but she could swear that it was implied. Mona squared her shoulders. "I'm not needy."

"No one said you were needy," he told her. This defensiveness was getting old. He was ready to be sympathetic, to talk or to listen, or just be there with her in total silence. But she had to stop beating him back every time he made a gesture. "Hell, Mona, I don't remember the chip on your shoulder ever being this big before."

Green lightning flashed from her eyes. "There *is* no chip on my shoulder."

Okay, he'd had enough. Unbuckling his seat belt, Joe shifted in his seat and gave it to her full blast.

"The hell there isn't. You could ram a hole in a brick building with that chip and still keep it in one piece. We're friends, remember?" he reminded her tersely. "Friends from way back. I was just offering you company if you wanted some."

"Well, I don't," Mona fairly snapped, then felt guilty about it. This was becoming an unfortunate pattern. Snapping, feeling guilty and then apologizing. If she could just manage to control her temper, she wouldn't be dancing this boring two-step with Joe over and over again. For some reason, he seemed to be the only one who could set her off like this, but that was no excuse for her acting like such a shrew.

"But I appreciate the offer," she said in a far more even tone. She didn't apologize to him outright, but she did try to explain her behavior. "A lot has happened in a short amount of time," she told him. With a sigh, she looked up at the sky outside the windshield. "I guess I was really hoping that nothing had changed while I was away. That I could just come back, pick up the reins of my life and slip back into it as if I'd never been gone—except that I'd be a lot better at diagnosing and taking care of animals," she added with a glimmer of a self-depreciating smile that came and went from her lips.

"That's not possible."

She closed her eyes and nodded. "I know."

No, she didn't, Joe thought. She'd misunderstood him.

"No, I mean, the part about you being a lot better at taking care of animals. If anyone ever had a gift for it, you do. Sometimes, I'd swear you even speak their language. You're better at it than any Apache I've ever known—but then," he remembered, "you are one-third Native."

His low-keyed praise made her smile. "You always did know how to make me feel better about things, even when you weren't trying." Smiling her appreciation, she said, "Thanks." Opening the door on her side, Mona climbed out of the Jeep, then turned to look at Joe one last time. "See you around, 'Sheriff.'"

He frowned. He'd forgotten about that for a moment. The title made him uncomfortable. It wasn't that he didn't think himself equal to the task. Ever since he'd turned over a new leaf all those years ago, he'd always done what needed to be done. He'd been a deputy for a number of years now and knew all the basic fundamentals of law enforcement in Forever.

The problem was he just didn't look forward to interacting with some of the citizens in Forever. The people who clung to drama and made mountains out of proverbial molehills. The ones who needed special kid-glove treatment. *Rick* was good at handling them, at returning Joanna Mendoza back to her home when she went for one of her moonlight walks in her flannel nightgown, sleepwalking with her eyes wide open.

Rick was equally as diplomatic tucking Charlie Halpern in for the night when the senior citizen had consumed more than he could comfortably imbibe and still walk a straight line. Rick had patience and knew how to talk to people like that.

Him, he hardly talked at all, unless it was to Mona and look how well *that* was going tonight. She snapped out every second sentence at him. That didn't exactly attest to his people skills.

"Offer still stands," he told Mona as she closed the passenger door behind her and began to walk away.

"I know."

And she did. She knew he was there for her, her own personal human safety net. That more than anything else urged her to behave like an adult. She didn't want Joe to know she needed him. Or to suspect the depths of her loneliness.

In response to his assurance, she didn't even bother turning around. Instead, she raised her hand over her head and waved at him as she continued walking up to her front door.

Had she been alone, she might have started whistling to keep herself company, but if she did that now, she knew Joe would take it as an indication that she was not up to facing the empty house. He had an annoying habit of being able to read her and guess what she was thinking. She didn't want to add this to his tally.

After letting herself in, Mona locked the door and began the process of turning on all the lights on the first floor. Granted it was a waste of energy, but it made her feel better. The light chased away the eerie shadows on the walls.

She was about to turn on the TV and leave it on a channel running an old movie—the voices would provide a form of company—when she heard someone knocking on the front door. Since the house was located on the outskirts of town, she doubted if this was a neighbor who had a sudden urge to call on her at this hour of the night. Or borrow a cup of sugar.

It had to be Joe.

Mona looked at her watch. It hadn't even been five minutes. She hadn't even had the opportunity to change out of her cocktail dress and get comfortable.

"I'm still fine, Joe!" she called out, raising her voice to compensate for the distance.

"Yeah, but he's not," she heard Joe say through the door.

"He?" she repeated. Mona quickly crossed the rest of the way to the door. "Who is 'he'?" she wanted to know as she unlocked the door and pulled it open. The next moment she had her answer.

Joe was holding a dirty, pathetically skinny, shaggy dog of dubious parentage in his arms. The dog looked frightened and far from happy. The whining sound he emitted wrenched her heart.

Mona never hesitated. All her better instincts instantly rose to the foreground. She took the dog from Joe and held the frightened animal against her chest, allowing the stray to absorb her warmth, to "sense" that he had nothing to be afraid of.

Speaking to the dog in a low, soft, soothing voice, she gently stroked his head. The whining subsided by degrees.

"Where did you find him?" she asked Joe.

"Right outside your house, in the street. Maybe he was coming to pay you a visit," he quipped, then grew a little more serious. "He was almost roadkill. I came this close—" he held the thumb and index finger of his right hand barely two inches apart "—to hitting him. He walked right in front of my Jeep. I swerved at the last second. I didn't see him before then." The downtrodden animal had been slinking by right in front of him, as if trying to avoid being noticed. "He doesn't have any tags and he's pretty dirty, so I'm guessing he's a stray. I thought that maybe you could check him out."

She was already won over. "Poor little guy," she murmured to the dog, still stroking him.

Though he'd stopped whining, he continued to shake even though she held him against her. Because he was severely underweight and seemed so frightened, Mona was fairly certain that someone had abused the animal severely. People like that, she thought angrily, should be filleted.

"You want to adopt him?" she asked Joe, since he'd brought the dog to her and asked her to check him out.

The question surprised him. Why would she think that? He liked his life simple. He believed that if a man had too many possessions, the possessions really had him. That especially applied to pets.

Joe wanted to own nothing. That way, there were no expectations, no disappointments. No ties to be severed if he wanted to pick up and leave.

"No," he answered. "But I thought that maybe you would."

Mona looked at him curiously. "Me?"

"Yeah."

From where he stood, it only made sense. Currently, Mona had no pet roaming around the house, a condition that he considered rather unusual for her. Growing up, Mona was constantly bringing home strays, nursing them back to health. Having a pet right now would definitely take the edge off of being alone.

"It's only logical," Joe argued. "How are people going to trust a vet with their pets if that vet doesn't even have a dog or a cat of her own?"

Mona laughed and shook her head. "Always looking out for me, aren't you?"

It was a teasing remark. She wasn't prepared for the seriousness of his expression—or of his tone—as Joe answered, "Yes, I am."

He meant it, she thought. The next moment she told herself not to make a big deal of it. He said a lot of things with that solemn look on his face. It was just his way. It didn't mean anything.

In any event, it wasn't so much a case of what Joe had just said, that people would regard her with suspicion if she didn't have a pet of her own. He probably believed that if she was busy nursing the dog, she would stop dwelling on the things that made her unhappy.

He was probably right, she mused.

Besides, she'd been on the lookout for a new pet ever since Lloyd, her beloved Labrador, had died six months ago at the age of thirteen.

Still cradling the stray against her, she looked up at Joe and quietly said, "Thank you."

And then she turned her attention to the animal. The mongrel was badly in need of a bath, but from what she could see at first glance, the dog didn't appear to be injured. Right now, her first order of business was to see about feeding him. Cleaning him up could wait.

"You hungry, Apache?" Mona asked her newfound friend.

Joe frowned, looking from the dog to her. "Apache?" he questioned. "You're actually going to call the dog Apache?"

Her smile widened. The smile infiltrated her eyes. "Yes."

"Why?" he asked, mystified.

"Because he *looks* like an Apache." Before Joe could say anything in protest to the comparison, she added pointedly, "Just look at the nobility in those eyes." She turned slightly so that the dog's face was more visible to Joe. "He's had his share of troubles and managed to survive and still come out whole. Still able to hold his head up high." She scratched the dog under his chin as she continued. The dog looked as if he'd just crossed over to heaven. "If that isn't a good description of an Apache, I don't know what is."

"You know, if you ever decide to stop being a vet, you could always become a politician."

Mona met his suggestion with a pronounced shiver. "God forbid. Anyway, I just got started finally putting all that veterinarian schooling to work. I don't plan to stop for another fifty, sixty years."

Mona didn't know the meaning of the word *stop,* Joe thought. She was relentless when she wanted something or had her mind set on an idea.

"If I know you, you'll just be getting your second wind by then," he said.

Tickled, Mona laughed, really laughed. As always, the sound got under his skin, doing things to him with an increased urgency that could easily turn out to be his undoing.

Time for him to get going. Before the temptation to stay grew to be too big to resist. Or conquered.

"I'll see you later," he said to Mona, then pet the dog's head. The dog didn't even seem to notice. His entire focus was on Mona. "You, too, 'Apache.'"

Just for a second, the dog shifted his eyes toward him, as if the animal sensed that was his new name. God, now Mona had him attributing a complex thought process to a dog.

With the dog still in her arms, Mona accompanied Joe the short distance to the door.

"Thank you for this," she said warmly, affectionately leaning her cheek against the top of Apache's caramel head.

Much as he would have liked to take the full credit for this, it was all just happenstance. The animal had picked the right time to cross his path. Two minutes either way and the dog would have still been roaming the streets.

Moving Apache over to her left side, Mona impulsively rose up on her toes and expressed her gratitude with a kiss.

She'd intended to kiss Joe on the cheek, but just before she made contact, Mona swayed, her balance shifting, and she suddenly wound up brushing her lips against his mouth instead. Memories of the first night she'd returned to Forever flashed through her head. The next second, heat pulsed through the rest of her.

The identical kind of heat, it turned out, that now wound its way through Joe. He'd felt it the instant her lips had touched his. Had there not been a dog between them, he might have been seriously tempted to push things further. Might have anchored her in place by taking hold of her upper arms with his hands and then brought her closer to him as he did his damndest to deepen the kiss.

To bond their souls a little more.

But the dog had started whining again, the jarring noise shattering the moment and the things that might have been.

Know just how you feel, Apache, he thought as he stepped back. It was obvious to him that the old adage about no good deeds going unpunished was true. Just as well. If he'd gone ahead and done what he'd wanted to do, there would be no end to the consequences.

The yearning he felt refused to go away. He did what he could to ignore it.

"If you need anything," he said to Mona, "just give me a call." Then, in case she took that to be some sort of open invitation to follow up on that fleeting kiss, he added, "I am the acting sheriff until your brother gets back, so it's my job to look out for everyone in Forever. You included."

She smiled at him. The smile seemed to pierce his chest and go straight into his heart. It was a damn silly notion considering the way he felt about complications.

"Nice to know." She raised Apache's paw and pretended that the dog was waving goodbye. Assuming a light-pitched voice she said, "'Thanks for not hitting me with your car, Sheriff Joe.'"

Joe said nothing. He merely rolled his eyes, turned on his heel and walked out.

The sound of her laughter, even after she closed the door, followed him down the short walkway and he could have sworn he heard it even as he got into the Jeep.

With determination, he started his car and pulled away, knowing that if he lingered even a second longer, he wouldn't be going anywhere except inside her home again.

And this time, the stray he'd be bringing to her would be him.

He had a feeling that this more than anything else was why Rick had left him in charge. The position was a safeguard against his acting impulsively. In other words, being acting sheriff was supposed to keep him on the straight and narrow. And that in turn meant that he couldn't allow himself to follow any basic instincts that reared their heads while Rick was gone.

"Think of everything, don't you, Rick?" he murmured under his breath, addressing his words to the man who was not there.

Chapter Ten

"Morning, Sheriff."

Alma and Larry's voices blended together in a sing-song cadence as Joe walked into the office the following day.

He had never cared very much for Mondays and this Monday promised to be a trying one.

Today was the day he assumed his new—albeit temporary, he silently emphasized—post.

Going toward his desk, he muttered a barely audible, "Morning, Alma. Morning, Larry," in response. He made his way around Larry.

Just before he was about to sit down, Alma placed herself between him and his chair.

Joe sighed. He'd already braced himself this morning, expecting to be the target of a great deal of ribbing today and probably for the next few days. Hopefully this wouldn't last the entire time the sheriff was gone, but to be honest, he wouldn't bet on it.

When Alma continued to place herself in his way even as he tried to move around her, he raised a quizzical eyebrow. "Yes?"

"You can't sit here," she told him, her heart-shaped face the picture of innocence.

It was going to be a *long* Monday. "And just why is that?"

"Because this isn't your desk right now." Turning, Alma pointed toward the small, crammed, glass-enclosed area that served as Rick's office. "That's where the sheriff sits," she informed him brightly.

Joe knew that if he gave even so much as an inch and allowed her to win this round, Alma and Larry were seriously going to ride roughshod over him. He intended to hand Rick back the office just the way that he had found it—running smoothly.

"That's where the sheriff sits when the sheriff is Rick," Joe corrected, then nodded toward his own desk. "And this is where the sheriff sits when the sheriff is me." He looked from one deputy to the other. Maybe it was better to cut to the chase right from the beginning. "Look, I don't like this any more than you do. Maybe even less, but leaving me in charge is something that Rick decided on his own, so let's just all try to get through it, okay?"

Larry grinned. "Who says we don't like it?" he asked. And then he laughed when Joe looked at him in confusion. "This gives us one hell of an opportunity to hold your butt to the fire."

Joe closed his eyes as he took his seat. "Now, there's a pretty image," he muttered.

Alma grinned wickedly. "Depends on what side of the fire you're on."

When he opened his eyes, Alma was still watching him.

"You do wear your jeans a whole lot better than Larry does," she told him, a wicked grin on her face.

"I take exception to that," Larry protested.

"Don't you two have work to finish?" Joe asked.

He heard the front door opening behind him and was grateful that Pete McKay chose that moment to walk into the sheriff's office.

For about ninety seconds.

It turned out Pete was there to file a complaint regarding the "noise pollution" he was forced to endure. Joe knew from experience that it wasn't the first time, but this time, he was in charge.

He listened to the retired hardware-store owner rant for a couple of minutes, sprinkling twenty-dollar words in between two-dollar phrases.

"You know, Pete, you might try talking like a regular person," Joe suggested patiently. He displayed no emotion one way or another. "It's not 'noise pollution,' it's a damn dog barking."

"It's a lot of damn dogs barking," the old man corrected angrily. "And it's getting worse."

Joe was fairly certain the problem wasn't getting worse because the noise was increasing. The reason lay elsewhere. "That's because you retired, Pete, and you're home all the time." He saw a reasonable solution. "Ever think of going back to work?"

"Can't," the old man bit off bitterly. He blew out an annoyed huff because he apparently had no one to blame for this but himself. If there had been someone else, Joe knew the old man would have loudly informed him of it. "I sold the hardware store to Jim Phelps last month."

Joe was aware that Larry and Alma were taking in every syllable while pretending to be busy.

He paused for a moment, thinking, then said, "Well, you could try offering to go back as a consultant." He saw Pete's sour look deepen. "I'm sure Jim could use you. There's a lot of stored-up knowledge in that head of yours, Pete," Joe said, laying it on thicker than he might have normally. "Why don't you ask him?"

Joe had a feeling that this display of even worse temper than usual was because the man, a lifelong bachelor with no family to speak of, had just recently retired and, devoid of hobbies, he had nothing to do with his days and nights. Every minor irritation grew to the size of a pending war.

Pete's frown grew so deep, it created ruts in his forehead. The old man waved an impatient hand, dismissing the suggestion. "Why bother? Phelps won't want me hanging around."

"Not hanging around, mentoring," Joe told him. He saw a flash of interest enter the man's dark gray eyes. "You could give advice, show people how things are done. Maybe even hold some do-it-yourself classes in the back of the store once in a while. I'll talk to Jim about it," Joe promised. "And in the meantime, I'll ask Doc if he could do something about the noise. Does that work for you?" he asked.

"Yeah." The snow-white head bobbed up and down as Pete appeared to consider what had just been said. "That works for me." Satisfied, Pete turned on his well-worn heels and headed for the door. He paused only long enough to say, "Thanks," before he closed the door behind him.

The moment the door clicked into place, Joe exhaled. He felt as if he'd just run a marathon. A long one. It took him a second to realize that instead of mercilessly tag-team ribbing him, Alma and Larry were applauding and giving him a standing ovation.

Alma stopped clapping and dropped her hands to her sides. "You know, I think that's the most I've ever hear you say at one time."

"At one time?" Larry echoed with a hoot. "Hell, that's the most he's ever said in a week. A month," he corrected.

Joe decided that he could do with some air—and some time away from his deputies. Getting to his feet, he reached for his hat that he'd tossed on the edge of his desk.

"Where're you going?" Larry asked.

Joe had never liked being questioned. Now was no exception. "I told Pete that I'd have a talk with Doc, so I'm going to go have a talk with Doc. That all right with you, Larry?"

Larry held his hands up as if he were surrendering and pretended to back away. "You're the boss, Joe."

"Ha!" was the only comment Joe made as he left the office.

He knew that Larry and Alma didn't really mean anything by the ribbing. They, and Rick, were as close to family as he had these days and this was what families did: they drove each other crazy. Except for his real family. They had gone out of their way to ignore him when he had been thrust into their midst, a recently orphaned ten-year-old boy.

Foregoing his Jeep, Joe opted to walk to the vet's. It was too beautiful a day not to enjoy at least some of it.

With his long stride, he got to Doc Whitman's fifteen minutes later. Years ago, Doc had bought the old Sutherland house and converted the bottom floor into an animal clinic. The veterinarian lived on the second floor. It had three bedrooms, but he kept two locked up for the most part, claiming to need very little in the way of space.

They had that in common, he and Doc.

McKay's house bordered the animal clinic on the left. There was enough room between the two buildings for any loud sounds coming from the clinic to be fairly muffled by the time they reached the old man's walls. Joe suspected that McKay had lodged the complaint because he just needed an excuse to come into the sheriff's office and interact with another human being.

Some people couldn't handle loneliness without it changing them. Joe had gotten fairly used to it himself. Until Mona had come back.

Joe blocked the thought and went up the front steps to the animal clinic's front door. As he did, he noted that McKay's 1983 Impala wasn't in his driveway. Hopefully, the old man had taken his advice and gone to see Jim Phelps about helping out at his former hardware store.

Knocking on the door, Joe walked into the clinic just as Shirley Hoffman exited one of the exam rooms, one arm draped over her daughter, Celeste's, shoulder. Celeste, twelve, was carrying her pet guinea pig, the obvious reason for the visit.

The visit had to have come out all right, Joe judged. The little girl was smiling.

Shirley paused at the empty receptionist's desk. The receptionist had decided last week to move to Seattle with her boyfriend and Doc had yet to find someone to take her place. Shirley put her purse on top of the desk and rummaged for her checkbook.

"How much do I owe you, Doctor?" she asked.

Her question was directed to Mona, who had come out behind her. Mona joined the woman, still making notes in the very thin folder she carried.

She wore a white lab coat and looked exceedingly professional—for Mona. The image of her, wearing the lab coat, high heels and nothing else, flashed through his mind.

The image stirred him.

"Nothing," Mona answered. When the woman looked at her quizzically, Mona explained, "The first visit is free."

"But this isn't our first visit," Shirley protested, although even from where he was standing, Joe could see that the woman looked hopeful.

"I meant, the first visit for me," Mona told her. She nodded toward the animal in the carrier that Celeste was holding. "Just make sure Ginny takes the medicine I gave you. She needs to take it until it's all gone," Mona emphasized.

That was when Shirley released the breath she was holding. "I don't know how to thank you. Celeste is so attached to that animal."

"No need for thanks, that's what I'm here for," Mona assured her, walking the pair out the front door.

"You're here to drive Doc to the poor house?" Joe asked after Shirley and Celeste were gone.

Aware that he was there, she'd acknowledged him with a nod until her business with Shirley and her daughter was finished. Now that they were alone, Mona was mildly curious what he was doing here.

"Shirley's husband lost his job last month," she told him. "They're having a tough time of it." She'd gotten that information from her brother as a quick review of what had been going on since she was last home. "Besides," she said with a careless shrug, "I'm only doing what Doc would do if he were here."

Joe realized that he'd missed that little fact. Ordinarily, Doc would have come out by now, drawn by the sound of voices if nothing else. "Doc's not here?" he questioned.

As she spoke, Mona began neatening the reception desk. With mail, flyers and folders scattered about, the surface currently resembled no-man's-land. "No."

"Where is he?" Joe pressed when she didn't elaborate beyond the one-word answer.

At times, he got the distinct feeling that she enjoyed pressing his buttons. All of them. At the same time.

"He drove over to the Jessup ranch first thing this morning. One of Drew Jessup's prize stallions is acting colicky."

Thinking of something she forgot to put down, she opened the folder she'd been writing in previously and made another notation. Finished, she left the folder neatly lying on top of the others. She intended to file them all away the first chance she got.

Joe was still standing there. Why? "I take it this isn't a social call."

"Pete McKay tried to lodge a formal complaint against Doc," he told her.

She'd been working here with Doc since the day after she'd arrived in Forever. That was a little over two weeks ago. And in that time, she'd noticed McKay standing in his yard, glaring over toward the clinic several times. Each time he wore an angry expression on his face.

"That grumpy old man would lodge a complaint against Mother Teresa if he got it into his head that he didn't like what she was doing," she said in disgust. His words replayed themselves in her head. She looked at Joe, confused. "Hey, wait a minute. You said 'tried.'"

"I did," he agreed, his voice giving nothing away.

"So why didn't he?" Mona asked.

He wasn't about to go into details, explaining that he'd suggested that McKay see the new owner of the hardware store and offer to give customers the benefit of his years of experience. Instead, Joe gave her a quick summary.

"Long story, but part of it is that I said I'd talk to Doc about seeing what he could do to keep the dogs from barking." Joe looked at her pointedly. "I figure now that you're around, that might not be such a problem anymore."

"And why is that? You think I'm going to gag the dogs?"

The image of her rushing about, slipping multicolored bandanas over the dogs' muzzles amused him, although he kept that image to himself. No sense in getting her annoyed. "I think that you're going to do whatever it is you do that makes them obey you and you're going to get them to keep quiet."

Her grandmother had called her an animal whisperer, but that had been just between the two of them. She doubted that Joe knew about that. "You're giving me a lot of credit."

"Only where it's due," he answered. She was good at getting animals to do what she wanted and they both knew it.

Joe took a look around, noticing the outer office for the first time since he'd gotten there. Scattered about the walls were framed photographs of a variety of animals, most of them with Doc standing beside them. He didn't recall ever seeing the photographs before. Not that he frequented the place all that much, but he'd been here a couple of times with Rick on business. The walls had been bare then.

"This your work?" he asked, turning back to her.

Over the years, as she'd worked with and learned from Doc, Mona had brought her camera along. It was an inexpensive, simple one but it accomplished what she wanted. It took pictures and captured memories. At the time, the photographs had been for her album. But recently, she decided that they also made good decorations.

"You might say that," she answered evasively.

"You took them?"

She smiled and nodded. "Yes."

"You framed them and hung them?" he continued.

"Yes," she answered, observing him carefully.

"Then, yeah, I 'might say that.'" He looked around

again, taking in the whole effect. "Nice touch," he told her.

She had no idea why his approval pleased her. Granted he was her friend, but she had always done her own thing without needing a seal of approval from anyone. Why did his create this warm glow inside of her?

"Thanks." She did her best to sound blasé. "I like it." She had to get back to work. There was a dog in back she needed to prepare to be neutered. Mona looked at him. "You want me to give Doc a message for you?"

She was telling him to leave, he thought. Just as well. He needed to get going. There was a patrol around town to make.

"No, I'll be back." One hand on the doorknob, he looked at her, reluctant to leave just yet. "How's Apache doing?" he asked.

The mention of her new pet brought a smile to the corners of her mouth. "Well, he didn't like getting a bath."

"Wouldn't think so." Although, the thought suddenly occurred to him, if he was the one being bathed by her, it wouldn't exactly qualify as a hardship.

He slanted a look in her direction, more than a little relieved that even though Mona was pretty intuitive, she didn't have the ability to read minds.

Mona had brought her new pet with her to the clinic, not wanting to leave him alone his first full day in new surroundings. For a moment, she thought about inviting Joe to come to the back and see the dog for himself. But he looked as if he wanted to get going and she did have a patient waiting for her, so she just told him about Apache rather than showed him.

"And he looks even thinner right now with all that dirt off, but he's eating," she said with affection.

Joe had no doubt of that. "Probably like the starving dog he is."

"Was," Mona corrected. "He can't possibly be starving after all the food he consumed between last night and this morning."

The dog had jumped up to reach the counter in the kitchen and wound up capturing what was left of a pot roast she'd made earlier in the week. She'd taken it out of the refrigerator to make a sandwich to take to work for lunch. She had to physically separate Apache from his "prey."

What amazed her was that the dog had allowed her to take the food away from him. It was proof that at bottom, Apache had a gentle nature. It also told her that she'd guessed right, he'd been abused and was fearful of punishment.

"The trick was to get him to stop eating before he exploded or ruptured something," she concluded.

"Not much of a trick for you," Joe said matter-of-factly. "Getting animals to behave and listen is right up your alley."

As far as she was concerned, getting animals to behave was just a given so she took no credit for it. "Thanks for bringing him to me." She had no doubt that the poor dog *would* have starved to death if Joe hadn't had the presence of mind to bring the animal to her.

Joe shrugged as if what he'd done was a no-brainer.

As if he'd been thinking only of the dog and not her when he decided to unite the two of them. "You're the town vet. Or one of them."

Mona had a strong suspicion that it had been more than that simple fact that made him decide to bring the poor thing to her, but she also felt that neither she nor Joe was comfortable exploring what had prompted him to do what he did. So she left his statement alone.

Instead, she cut the conversation short with words meant to send him on his way. "I'll tell Doc you were looking for him when he gets back."

He nodded. "No hurry." Joe opened the door. "I just wanted to let him know that Pete was complaining, but I think I handled it."

Now he had succeeded in arousing her curiosity. The dog awaiting surgery could wait another couple of minutes. "Oh? How?"

"Pete sold his business a short while ago. He's got more time on his hands than he's used to and nowhere to go now that he doesn't have to work. I got him to offer his services to Jim now that Phelps owns the hardware store. This way, he's got something to do and isn't hanging around his house, listening for the next dog to bark."

She nodded, impressed that Joe actually put himself in someone else's shoes. He was more intuitive than she remembered. "Doc'll be relieved to hear that. He doesn't like dealing with complaints."

Joe was about so say something else, but any further conversation was curtailed by the arrival of a frantic Dana Richards who clutched what sounded like an asthmatic cat to her more than ample bosom.

"Mr. Boots stopped breathing twice this morning," she cried. The Siamese cat seemed to have great difficulty getting in air.

It looked like Dakota, the mixed-breed dog in the back, had just gotten a stay of execution for his manhood, Mona thought.

"I'll see you, Joe," she said, before turning to the distraught woman. "Let's go to exam one," she coaxed Dana, placing a comforting arm around the woman's shoulders.

Joe left then. As he closed the door, the same unbidden thought he'd had earlier flashed through his mind. Mona, in the white lab coat, wearing high heels and nothing else but a smile.

He felt his blood heating as he walked back to the sheriff's office to get his Jeep. The fast pace he'd assumed had nothing to do with it.

He made a mental note to start taking cold showers instead of warm ones.

Chapter Eleven

"There she is," Miss Joan declared with a broad, satis-fied smile as Mona came into the diner. The unofficial town psychologist beckoned her over and then pointed to the only empty table in the place. "Pull up a booth and sit down," she coaxed, tendering the invitation as if she hadn't said the exact same thing last night, and the night before that.

Mona had shown up at the diner for dinner that first Monday that Rick and Olivia had left for their hon-eymoon. Her appearance had been prompted by her decision that she preferred grabbing a bite to eat at the diner and listening to the snatches of various conversa-tions around her to going directly home. The house still mocked her with its emptiness.

Although it wasn't exactly empty. Apache did come home with her every night after spending the day at the animal clinic. And once across the threshold, the scrappy dog made enough noise for three. It was obvi-ous that he was happy to be away from the animals that were brought to the clinic. She'd quickly learned that Apache preferred humans to his four-footed brethren.

When she came into the diner, initially Miss Joan

had told her to leave Apache outside, tethered to the first handy stable item she could find. But that was because Miss Joan was accustomed to dogs behaving like her own pet, an enormous dog who had an appetite for the convertible tops of sports car and whatever else he could sink his teeth into—literally.

But Apache, with his desperate need to be loved, had won Miss Joan over within the space of an hour. By day two, he was allowed—invited, really—to come inside the diner with no hesitation.

"So, what can I get for you and your fierce guard dog today?" Miss Joan asked, abandoning the cloth she used to massage her clean counter.

Mona spared a glance at the dog who followed her like a short, fuzzy shadow, running her hand over his head affectionately.

"Just some soup for me and the usual for Apache," Mona told the woman.

Miss Joan smiled. "The usual it is."

"The usual" was the biggest bone that was available to gnaw on. Miss Joan took it upon herself to serve the dog personally, amused by the way the animal first licked her hand when she set the bone in front of him before settling in to enjoy his feast.

After bringing today's offering to the pet, the woman chuckled to herself as she rose again to her feet.

"If my first husband, Clyde, had reacted that way when I gave him dinner, we'd still be married." About to go back behind the counter, Miss Joan paused as she scrutinized Mona. "Not feeling well, honey?" the woman asked, lowering her voice as she put the question to her. When Mona eyed her quizzically, the woman explained, "Most folks don't ask for soup unless they're feeling kind of under the weather."

"No, I'm fine." Mona deliberately put a little bounce in her voice. "I just felt like having some of your chicken soup. It really is good."

Miss Joan beamed, pleased despite the fact that she wasn't fooled. "Flattery'll get you everywhere," she said, and went back to the kitchen to bring out a bowl of the soup.

Mona watched the older woman go through the swinging door into the kitchen and slowly sighed. She wasn't being strictly honest with Miss Joan. She wasn't ill, but it was more than just good taste that prompted her to order soup for dinner. She hoped that the warmth of the soup would somehow ease the emptiness that she felt inside.

She'd thought—hoped—that she had finally conquered the feeling because it had disappeared for several days. But then, just like that, the emptiness returned, coming out of nowhere and threatening to swallow her up whole if she didn't find a way to beat it back again.

In the midst of work—and today had been a particularly hectic day—she felt alone. Even here, in the diner, she felt the emptiness eating away at her despite the fact that this was dinnertime and a great many people, travelers as well as town citizens, were clustered here, filling every available seat in the place except for her table.

She had a feeling that Miss Joan had saved the booth for her and she was grateful. She knew if she said anything, or made any mention of her gratitude, Miss Joan would tell her that she had no idea what she was talking about.

Miss Joan was like that.

The woman returned with her soup, steam curling from the bowl and melding with the air above it, and placed it on the table in front of her.

Mona smiled as brightly as she could as she fought back the crippling ache. What *was* the matter with her? she silently demanded, annoyed with herself. "Thank you, Miss Joan."

The woman nodded, sweeping away the thanks. "Anything else, honey?" she wanted to know.

Mona shook her head. "Nothing I can think of." After all, Miss Joan could do nothing about this feeling eating away at her the way Apache was eating away at his bone.

But rather than make her way back behind the counter and other customers, Miss Joan looked at her for a long moment. Looking, it felt, right *through* her.

"You sure about that, honey?" Miss Joan finally asked her.

Mona forced a very worn smile to her lips, doing her very best to make it seem spontaneous and natural. "I'm sure."

Just then, the door to the diner opened and Joe walked in. He removed his hat the moment he crossed the threshold, then slowly looked around, searching for a seat. All the stools that lined the counter were taken and so were, it appeared, all the booths.

With a resigned sigh, Joe began to put his hat back on. But before he could leave again, Miss Joan saw him and picked up her voice by several decibels.

Raising her hand to catch his attention, she called out, "Over here, Joe." Miss Joan shifted her glance toward Mona and asked what anyone could easily see was a rhetorical question as far as she was concerned. "You don't mind sharing a table with Joe, do you, honey?"

Actually, she did. Right now, Mona wasn't feeling at her best. She felt dull tonight and she couldn't put her finger on exactly *what* had triggered this feeling, but she felt that she would make awful company.

However, she knew that it would do no good to protest or worse, take exception to Miss Joan's seating plan. Miss Joan was one of those people who always knew best, or so the older woman liked to believe.

As for her, Mona had too much regard for the diner owner to even make an attempt at refusing her.

"No, I don't mind," Mona murmured, more to herself than to Miss Joan.

"Here, boy, take a load off," Miss Joan instructed, gesturing him into the booth seat opposite Mona. "So what can I get you, Joe?" As she had done with Mona, Miss Joan peered closer at his face. "You look tired, Joe. Some kind of crime wave hit Forever?" the woman asked, an amused glimmer in her eyes.

"Not tonight," he told her, deliberately not going into any details regarding why he looked as if he hadn't slept much the past few days.

The woman was, among other things, not just the owner of the diner and a budding psychologist, but what amounted to the town crier, as well. A person with that many so-called hats to wear had no need to know that the woman she just sat him with was the one responsible for his sleeplessness.

Things were getting worse in that respect, not better. Rather than taking her presence in stride the way he thought he would, having Mona around like this, interacting with her a little almost everyday, just made him acutely aware of the fact that he wanted her. A great deal.

And Mona, undoubtedly, had other plans for herself. There wasn't an endless supply of men in Forever, but there were enough and he'd seen several coming by the clinic with pets or borrowed animals, obtained from helpful friends or well-meaning relatives, just to have an excuse to confer with the sexiest veterinarian east of California.

It was only a matter of time before one of those guys put a lock on her affections, and then that would be the end of it. He would have to terminate his own longing at that point. Hell, maybe *then* he'd start getting a decent night's sleep.

Or, if not by then, he definitely would by the time Mona became Mrs. Somebody-or-Other because then he would go on being just Joe, good at his job and undistracted by extraneous things—like the laugh of a beautiful veterinarian who popped up in his fantasies with frustrating regularity.

"Just get me a ham and cheese on rye, black coffee and a piece of that cherry pie of yours," Joe requested in response to Miss Joan's query.

Mona glanced toward the counter and saw the empty cake container where the cherry pie was usually kept on display for the customers.

"Looks like they're out of cherry pie, Joe," she commented.

Miss Joan placed a hand on his shoulder and gave it a squeeze. "Don't you worry that handsome head of yours," she told Joe. "I figured you'd be coming in tonight and I set a piece aside for you." She looked at Mona. "He orders the same dessert every night. I'd do the same for you if you were predictable—or ate dessert," Miss Joan threw in over her shoulder as she walked away from them and toward the counter again.

"If you'd rather eat alone," Joe began, "I can just get mine to go."

"And disappoint Miss Joan?" Mona asked. "I don't think so. The woman looked as if she was a fairy god-mother at loose ends, doing her best to make something 'happen' between us," Mona said with the first smile she felt like offering today.

He did that for her, she thought. Joe made her smile for no reason at all. To counterbalance that, he could also arouse her temper faster than anyone else, a temper whose magnitude she wasn't even aware of until Joe popped into the picture.

"I don't think she needs to make anything happen," Joe told her quietly, his eyes on hers.

Mona looked at him sharply. Was he saying that she was wrong in her supposition, or that something was *already* happening between them and they didn't need Joan to stir the pot?

Joe's tone, as well as his reply, confused her and for the life of her, Mona couldn't sort out what he actually meant.

Or maybe she was afraid to.

So she answered him with as much evasiveness as possible. "I'm fairly sure that Miss Joan wouldn't be of the same opinion as you if you asked her."

"Miss Joan marches to the beat of her own drum," he agreed. There was a faint smile in his voice as he added, "But then, so do you."

She was about to ask him just what he meant by that when he turned his attention to the dog at her feet. Apache appeared oblivious to everything and everyone around him as he went wholeheartedly at the bone Miss Joan had placed before him.

"How're you doing, boy?" Joe asked, leaning down to scratch the animal behind the ears.

Apache paused for less than half a second to look up at the intruding human before resuming his determined gnawing. Joe straightened up and faced Mona again.

"He looks happier," he told her. "Also wider." He laughed, amused. "You did a good job with him."

Mona was about to point out the very obvious fact that she was *supposed* to be able to do a "good job" getting the dog healthy again considering that she was, after all, a vet, but somehow, that sounded pretty argumentative even to her own ears. So instead, she just rendered a careless, one-shoulder shrug and murmured a simple, "Thanks."

Miss Joan returned with Joe's dinner, offering the temporary sheriff a wide smile, then shifting her keen gaze to include Mona.

"Here you go. Sandwich, coffee and pie," Miss Joan announced as she slide each plate and cup from the tray she'd brought onto the table. Finished, she tucked the tray under one arm. "All right, now get to it," the woman instructed. Again she spared a glance in Mona's direction. "Both of you."

And just like that, Mona could feel her cheeks heating, taking on a hue all their own. To her recollection, she'd never blushed before. Not even when she'd had what she now freely admitted was a *stupid* fling with Steven James during her second year in college. She'd known from the beginning that she wasn't in love with the extremely good-looking senior, but it was college and she was away from home, free to test the waters of independence. So she had.

Besides, like most of the girls around him, she'd found herself exceedingly attracted to Steven.

Or so she'd thought at the time.

But the attraction she'd felt back then was an empty one involving merely Steven's looks and nothing of a deeper substance. Steven James, it turned out, didn't *have* a deeper substance. What she saw was not only what she got, but it was apparently all there was to the pre-med student.

It took coming home and running into Joe over and over again to make her see the difference. There was no denying that she was attracted to Joe, that she felt more than just a spark of electricity whenever she was around him. But that attraction encompassed not just his dark good looks, but the man, as well. Though she wasn't about to voice it out loud, Joe Lone Wolf was a good, decent man with qualities that made him good-looking inside, as well as out.

"Heard from Rick?" Joe asked her after several seconds of silence wrapped in the surrounding din had ticked by.

Mona nodded. She had, earlier in the week. "Just a postcard that said 'No offense, but glad you're not here.'" She nodded toward him. "You get anything?" she asked.

He took a long sip of his bracing coffee. Resting his cup, he shook his head. "No, but then, I didn't expect to. A man on his honeymoon doesn't spend his time thinking about the job he left behind. Right now, he's probably squeezing the last drop of pleasure out of the honeymoon. He's due back in a couple of weeks," he added matter-of-factly.

"I know."

And once Rick and Olivia and the almost-baby were back, she was going to have to figure out where to go. Pronto, Mona thought.

So far, the whole thing was up in the air. She'd shelved it and promptly forgot about looking into the matter. She hadn't thought about having to move since the evening of the wedding.

The evening Joe had brought Apache into her life, she remembered with a fond smile, glancing down at her dog. Apache was making short work of the bone.

Mona supposed that she had better *start* thinking about it, about finding a new place to stay, and soon. The Murphy place might be an option, but only after it was fixed up.

Maybe she could crash at Doc's for a while, she thought. He had that big old house and lived in only the kitchen and one bedroom. She could easily rent one of the free bedrooms.

Most likely, she'd have to threaten him to take the money. Doc was like that, charitable to a fault. He'd probably say that at his age, he didn't have a whole lot of use for money. She'd have to remind him that the clinic could always use more expansion, or a new MRI machine. He couldn't turn down the money then, she thought confidently.

Joe broke into her thoughts by asking her out of the blue, "What are we doing here, Mona?"

She blinked, confused by the question. Wasn't it obvious? "What?"

He didn't say anything to enlighten her about his meaning. Instead, he just repeated his question. "I said, what are we doing here?"

"Eating?" she guessed, her voice going up a little the way it did when she felt herself on unsafe ground. "Talking a little," she added. She cocked her head, looking at him and waiting for him to elaborate.

What he meant was what were they doing, sitting around playing games, pretending that this "something" shimmering between them didn't exist. But instead of saying as much, he got to the heart of the matter because it was time to get things moving and there would never be a better time.

Setting down his fork on the near-empty plate, he dove in.

"Mona, I'd like to ask you out for a date."

"A date," she repeated incredulously. Her pulse suddenly accelerated into triple time. She tried to tell herself that it was because the soup was hot and she'd just almost burned her tongue. But even she realized just how lame that really sounded.

"Yes, a date," Joe underscored. He wondered if he'd just made a stupid mistake he would live to regret, or if the regret would come because he hadn't taken this chance.

"You mean, like when a man and a woman go some place to eat and talk?" Mona asked innocently, deliberately shifting her gaze to the food between them and then back up to his face.

"Yes," he answered tersely, refusing to back away. You never knew what you were missing if you didn't try. His mother had said that to him the day before she'd died. "The only difference is that they go in together and leave together. And the guy pays," he added as an afterthought.

"Not always," Mona contradicted, clinging to her perverseness as if it was a protective shield. "In this day and age—"

Exasperated, Joe rose in his seat, leaning into her. Taking her startled face in his hands, he kissed her. Long and hard.

When he drew back again an eternity later, the diner had tilted a little. But he wasn't paying attention to the diner. He was paying attention to the woman who had begun to haunt his dreams. Again.

Stunned, a little shocked, Mona waited for the electricity to stop shooting through her veins. It didn't seem to want to.

"What did you do that for?"

"The primary reason was to shut you up—it worked beautifully," he pointed out needlessly. "The other reason, well, I think you know what the other reason is. And if you don't," he added, settling back in his seat, "then I did it wrong."

This was where a flippant answer would fit in nicely, she thought. All she had to do was say it and things would go back to the way they'd been.

Not a single flippant statement occurred to her.

"No, you didn't do it wrong," she told him quietly, her eyes on his. "You did it exactly right."

Mona realized that she said what she had, messing up her chances for a successful retreat, because she didn't want things to go back to the way they'd been.

At least, not yet.

Chapter Twelve

She had a date.

A date with Joe.

The thought still mystified Mona the next day. Joe would to swing by after work and pick her up at the house. And they were going to Miss Joan's—because it was the only available place to go—and have dinner.

Nothing they hadn't done before. Singularly. The difference this time was that they would do it together. On purpose, not because Miss Joan had suddenly taken it upon herself to seat one of them with the other for lack of space. Or because she'd suddenly decided that they would make a good couple.

Joe wanted to take her out.

Mona caught herself humming more than once during the course of the day. When her stomach wasn't tied up in knots.

Neither reaction made any sense to her. This was Joe she was going out with. Joe, whom she'd known since she was a teenager. Going out with him, date or not, should be a piece of cake. Old hat. Nothing to get excited about. Certainly nothing to get nervous about.

And yet she was both.

Because this was also Joe, the guy she'd had a crush on all those years ago.

Work had always helped her cope with mental unrest. Today was one of those days where being busy would have been a blessing. But unfortunately, no blessings in the offing today. There had been only two appointments that morning and only one walk-in.

As a result, the minutes dripped away slowly. That afternoon, Simon Taggert had called Doc about his quarter horse, Wildfire. The animal had gotten tangled in some barbed wire, panicked and cut up two of his legs trying to get free. Doc had left for Taggert's ranch immediately.

"Hold down the fort, Mona," were Doc's parting words to her, thrown over his shoulder, as he hurried out to his truck.

The problem with that was that there was nothing to hold down. The "fort" was almost painfully empty. There was only one animal, a cat, in the hospital area. The pet was staying overnight. Mittens was recovering from yesterday's emergency surgery. The willful feline had apparently decided to snack on a long section of wool that was originally intended to become part of a sweater Mittens' mistress was knitting. The wool had gotten entangled around her intestines. The surgery had been exceedingly challenging and, thankfully, successful.

But that had been yesterday. Today involved periodic checking to see how the cat was doing. Mittens was doing fine, which was more than Mona could say for herself. Attacks of antsiness had her all but climbing the walls.

There was no reason to feel this way, she kept arguing. This was the same Joe she'd always known. The only thing that had changed since she'd gone away to college was that he had grown handsomer and just possibly more silent.

The only actual "business" that had transpired at the animal clinic today occurred when Greta Wilson had come in to buy Alec, her border collie, his six-month supply of heart medicine.

Mona hated being at loose ends and not accomplishing anything. She knew she had to act fast or wind up going crazy before her date even started. So, with Apache following her around like an extension of her shadow, Mona set about straightening the clinic and washing and cleaning everything in sight—whether it needed it or not.

The frenzy took her a little over two hours. Finished, Mona sat back, waiting for Doc to return. Since there was only the cat in the back to occasionally monitor, she decided that she'd go home early and get ready. Maybe take a hot bath in an attempt to take the edge off her nerves.

She glanced at her watch. Doc had been gone for some time now. Since he hadn't called her, she felt that the injured quarter horse must be in good shape. And that in turn meant that Doc should be back pretty soon.

Just then, the floorboard directly overhead creaked. Mona looked up and stared at the ceiling. The floor didn't creak unless someone was walking on it. Had he gotten back earlier and gone directly upstairs for some reason? Was he sick?

Ordinarily, when Doc returned from a call, he walked into the clinic. Maybe he'd taken the side stairs and gone up to take care of something. She was pretty certain that if he wasn't feeling well, he would have called by now.

If he was here, that meant she could go home. But Mona didn't want to leave without telling him that she was going.

She gave it a few minutes. But when the time passed and Doc still hadn't come down into the clinic, she decided it was time that Mohammed went up the stairs to see the mountain.

She picked up her purse and checked to make sure she had her keys.

There was a staircase in the back just to the side of the operating area that led to the second floor. Rather than hang back behind her as she made her way up, Apache crowded her on each step, reaching the landing at the same time she did.

"Doc? Are you up here?" Mona called out when she didn't see him. He didn't answer. Curious, she ventured forth a little farther. She didn't like the idea of invading his privacy, especially if he wasn't there, but she was *sure* she'd heard footsteps overhead. "I thought I heard you walking around and I wanted to let you know that I was leaving early today. Doc?" she called again, raising her voice when he still didn't answer.

The house was old and sections of boards beneath the neutral-colored carpet creaked. If Apache hadn't stayed at her side all day, she would have blamed the noise on him. The dog had gone exploring around the building a couple of times and he'd managed to wander into the living quarters twice. Doc had brought him down, chuckling and telling her that she had an explorer on her hands.

The "explorer" was still right here, next to her.

Feeling unaccountably uneasy, Mona went from room to room. Since Doc hadn't answered her, she decided that he wasn't in his rooms. But what—or who—was?

When she tried to open the door to the third and last bedroom, she discovered that it was locked. From the inside. Something cold and icy slid down her spine. Unless raccoons had suddenly learned how to lock doors, someone had broken into Doc's house. And whoever it was was hiding in the bedroom.

Thank God she was the one who'd discovered this. She couldn't bear the thought of Doc stumbling onto the intruder and possibly getting hurt or shot by him. Knowing Doc, he'd be tempted to feed the thief and give him a place to sleep. Kindness wasn't always repaid with kindness. Doc was entirely too trusting.

Angry at this intrusion, Mona raised her voice. "I've got the sheriff downstairs," she informed the person she was certain was on the other side of the locked door. "All I have to do is call out and he'll be up here in a second. With his gun. Why don't you just unlock the door and tell me what you're doing here?"

After a moment, she heard the lock being turned. And then, ever so slowly, the door opened. The person in the room answered her question as she walked out. "Waiting for Doc to come back."

The world around Mona went in and out of focus twice, alternating between just blurred edges and a complete blur. She tried to tell herself she was seeing things.

Except that she wasn't.

"Why are you here?" she heard herself asking the dark, petite woman with the large brown eyes. She struggled to keep her voice low.

Mona felt as if the other woman's eyes were all but devouring her. "I just told you, I'm waiting for—"

Mona cut her off impatiently. "No, why are you *here?* Here in Forever? You were supposed to leave. At the wedding, you said you were leaving."

"No," Elena Ruiz corrected softly. "*You* said I was leaving. I just walked away because I didn't want to cause a scene at Enrique's wedding."

As if her showing up hadn't already lain the groundwork for that, Mona thought angrily. "He goes by Rick," Mona informed her curtly. Anger melded with contempt as she said, "You don't even know that."

"How could I?" Elena cried, frustrated. "He won't talk to me. *You* won't talk to me."

And she didn't want to be talking to her now. "All the more reason for you to go," Mona pointed out in exasperation.

Elena almost pleaded as she said, "But I can't make amends if I go."

"There's nothing you can do to make amends so you might as well go," Mona told her coldly.

She hated this, hated confrontations, hated being in the same room with a woman who hadn't cared for anyone but herself for so long. And now she was back, expecting to be forgiven and embraced? Just like that?

"Doc thinks I can make amends," Elena told her. It

was evident that hope was all she had to cling to. "He thinks that you and Enr—Rick will come around."

"Not for at least a hundred years—" And then she stopped as Elena's words replayed themselves in her head. "What's Doc got to do with it?" she asked. "And what are you doing in his house?" The strays Doc dealt with were the four-legged kind, not two legged. Why was this woman in his house? In one of his bedrooms?

"Doc's letting me stay here until I can find a way to prove to you and your brother how deeply, deeply I regret walking away from you." She reached out to place her hand on Mona's arm, but Mona jerked back, putting herself out of reach.

"Rick said you didn't walk away, you ran," Mona corrected. Her eyes narrowed as she got down to what was bothering her about all this. "Doc's a good man, he knows how I feel about the situation. About you." He wouldn't hurt her like this, sheltering Elena when he knew how much the woman's rejection had hurt her. "What did you threaten him with to make him let you stay in his house?" Mona demanded.

Elena pressed her lips together. For a moment, it appeared as if her thoughts were elsewhere. "Yes, I know he's a good man. A very good man." She let out a shaky breath. "I should have realized that a long time ago, too. And no matter what you think of me, I didn't threaten him. I couldn't. Staying in his house was Doc's idea."

Her mother's tone suggested things that she didn't want to hear. Didn't want to think about. But despite her denial, Mona knew that it would eat away at her until she had the truth. Right now, her imagination made her think the worst.

"Is Doc a friend of yours?" Mona couldn't bring herself to add to the question, to give Elena an alternative to choose from. As it turned out, she didn't have to.

"Doc would have been the best thing to happen to me—if only I had let him."

Mona shattered inside. She wanted to scream at Elena, to accuse her of lying. But the look on the woman's face verified everything for her. Mona didn't want to hear anymore. She felt angry and betrayed. Betrayed by one of the few people she'd ever allowed herself to trust.

How could he? How *could* he?

She ran out of the room. Behind her, she could hear Elena calling her name, but Mona didn't turn around. She flew down the stairs with Apache anxiously right behind her.

Mona didn't stop running once she got to the first floor. Instead, she kept going, blindly making her way out the front door. That was when she plowed right into Doc. Because he was so much larger and heavier than she was, Mona found herself stumbling backward from the impact.

Stunned, Doc caught her by the shoulders to steady her. "Mona, where are you going to in such an all-fired hurry?"

She angrily shrugged him off. "Let go of me!" she ordered.

Concern leaped into his eyes. "Mona, what's wrong? What happened? Why are you running away from the clinic?" Doc glanced through the open door and toward the rear of the clinic as he tried to understand her strange behavior. "Did something happen with Mittens?"

"The cat's fine," she bit off. "But I'm not." There was hurt and anger in her eyes as she glared at him. "I trusted you, Doc. I *trusted* you," she repeated with angry emphasis. "You were the father I never had. How could you?" she cried. "How could you do this to me?"

For a moment, he seemed completely confused. And then he understood. "You went upstairs."

"Yes, I went upstairs," she spat out. "How long has that woman been hiding here in your house?" Mona asked. "Since the wedding?"

"Yes," Doc answered in a heavy, solemn tone. "Mona, she's your mother. Please, give her a chance. For both your sakes."

"She's not my mother," Mona cried. "Abuela was my mother," she insisted. "That woman you took into your home is a complete stranger. I don't know her—"

"Then get to know her," Doc interrupted, trying to get through to her. "You have to try, Mona. Elena's been through a lot—"

He was taking *her* side. Mona went numb inside. "Yeah, well, so have I."

She didn't want to hear anymore, didn't want to argue about this. Didn't even want to think that this was happening. Mona spun around on her heel and ran away from the clinic she'd been more than ready to work in for so long. Without making a sound, Apache ran out the door right behind her.

Mona didn't stop running until she got to her car. Getting in, she waited only long enough for the dog to jump into the backseat. Mona slammed the door shut and peeled out of the small parking lot.

In her rearview mirror, she saw Doc standing where she'd left him, watching her go. He appeared upset.

"That makes two of us, Doc," she whispered.

Hot tears stung her eyes as she drove away.

SHE HAD NO IDEA HOW LONG she'd been standing there, in the cemetery, talking to the headstone that she and her brother had bought for her grandmother.

Pouring out her heart to the memory of the woman the way she hadn't since she was a little girl.

On automatic pilot when she'd left the clinic, she didn't realize she was driving in this direction until she'd almost reached the cemetery.

Ordinarily, whenever she was upset, whenever something was really bothering her, coming out here to talk it out with her grandmother seemed to help. Right now, as she talked to the headstone, Mona could almost envision her small, gray-haired grandmother sitting there, a solemn expression on her face, listening to her. When she was done, Abuela would advise her. The old woman's advice was sparingly given out, but it had always made her feel that everything was going to be all right.

But now there was no low-key, gravelly voice to tell her what direction to take, or to say just the right words that would put her dilemma into the proper perspective.

Mona felt incredibly lonely. Incredibly lonely and betrayed.

"What do I do, Abuela? How can I ever forgive her for what she did? How can I forgive him?" Doc knew how she felt about the woman he'd taken in. How could he have done that? And how could he now ask her to give her a chance? Especially since what he was asking her to do was forgive the woman and start fresh?

"You know, this wasn't what I pictured when I suggested we go out on a date."

A second ago, she was the only one in the cemetery. The voice, coming out of nowhere, made her jump and gasp. The next second, she looked down accusingly at Apache. At the very least, she would have expected the dog to bark and warn her of Joe's approach.

No bark, no warning. All Apache did was run up to Joe and enthusiastically wag his tail as if he hadn't seen his rescuer in at least a hundred years. The dog's tail thudded against the neighboring headstone, beating out what sounded like a rhythmic tattoo.

Joe blew out a breath, proceeding very cautiously. Despite all her bravado, he knew that Mona was very fragile right now. When he hadn't found her at home, he thought she was still at the clinic. He assumed some kind of emergency had come up. No problem, he was willing to wait.

But when he arrived at the clinic, he discovered that she had fled. Doc had filled him in on what had happened. It wasn't all that hard finding her after that. When Mona felt as if her world was coming apart at the seams, she always came here, to the cemetery, to talk to her grandmother. And search for peace.

Averting her face, afraid that another tear might betray her, Mona murmured. "I'm sorry. I forgot about our date."

"Good thing I don't have an ego to bruise," he said lightly, poking fun at himself in an attempt to get her to come around. He'd just given her a straight line. When she said nothing, he gave it one final beat, then said quietly, "Doc told me what happened."

Tears all but choked her. Mona looked in his direction, struggling not to cry. But her eyes were welling up anyway.

"How could he, Joe?" she cried, wanting desperately to understand, to come up with a reason she could understand and forgive. "How could he do that to me? How could he take her in, knowing how I felt? I *trusted* him and he took her side."

Very slowly, Joe drew closer to her by degrees, approaching her the way he would a wounded animal. Because that was what she was. Wounded. And he wanted nothing more than to help her heal.

"Doc wasn't taking sides, Mona, you know that. You know *him*. He just wants to help the two of you heal a rift."

"This isn't a rift," she retorted. "Friend have arguments, they get mad, they don't talk for a couple of days. That's a rift. *This* is a chasm," she informed him with emphasis. "You don't put a Band-Aid on a chasm and hope it'll all get better."

"Not unless you have one hell of a Band-Aid," he quipped. And then he looked at her pointedly. "Or one hell of a heart, willing to forgive."

"My heart's the usual size," Mona answered, still

struggling not to cry. "And right now, it's not feeling very forgiving."

Joe had managed to cut the distance between them down to a mere couple of inches. Enough to be able to put his arms around her and hold her to him just as the dam broke open inside her.

"I'm not supposed to cry," she sobbed against his shoulder, unable to stop.

"Don't worry," he told her softly as he tightened his arms around her, willing her to be comforted. "I'm not going to tell."

She broke down completely at that.

Chapter Thirteen

Mona hoped that if anyone from the town drove by and saw her crying like this in the cemetery, they would think her tears were for the woman whose body rested in peace beneath the headstone.

There was no reason why anyone would guess that it was because she felt so betrayed by both the man she'd thought of as her surrogate father and the woman who had given birth to her, then took herself out of her life.

But no one drove by and no one knew she was crying except for the dog that stood like a sentry right beside her.

And Joe.

Desperately trying to get a grip on herself—crying never solved anything—and feeling as if she was dehydrated, utterly drained of any and all moisture, Mona drew her head back. She gazed up at Joe, whose arms were still very much around her, creating a shelter for her to cling to.

It was merely an illusion, she told herself, trying not to allow herself to believe it was anything more than that. But still, the idea helped her cope.

By degrees, she became aware of the front of his shirt and what she'd done to it. "I'm sorry, I got your shirt all wet."

The price to pay was infinitesimally small for having her in his arms. He just wished that she wasn't so terribly distressed. Ordinarily, he left people their dignity, allowing them to cope with whatever it was that upset them. But this was Mona. There was no such option here.

"Fortunately, it's wash and wear," he quipped, then added, "Don't worry about it."

Joe knew what this was about, what had made her crumple this way and he wanted to make it all better. He wanted to make her see what he assumed Doc saw, as well. That by allowing her mother back into her life, by forgiving her, Mona would be a great deal happier and it would help to erase her residual pain and resentment.

But this wasn't a time for lectures, however well-intentioned. She wouldn't be receptive to any speeches about her mother right now. Mona was about to pull away, like one of the wounded animals she treated.

"C'mon," he urged, slipping his arm around her shoulders and turning toward the front of the cemetery. "I'll take you home." They could go out to dinner some other time. Mona came first.

She shook her head, although she didn't pull away from him. Having him here soothed her. With Rick gone and Doc's betrayal, Joe was the only one she could still trust. The only real friend she could count on.

"You don't have to," she told him. "My car's parked out front."

Joe really didn't want her driving anywhere in her present condition. She was far too overwrought to be by herself.

"I'll have Larry or Alma bring it over tomorrow morning in time to get you to work," he promised. With his arm still around her shoulders, he gently steered her toward the cemetery entrance.

Too drained and exhausted to argue and more than a little afraid to be alone with her thoughts, Mona let him guide her.

"I don't know if I'm going to work tomorrow," she told Joe, struggling to keep her voice even. To keep the tears out. If she began to cry again, she wouldn't be able to stop.

Joe made no comment until she got into his vehicle. Taking care to get Apache into the backseat, he then rounded the Jeep's hood and got in on his side.

This was serious, he thought. Mona had wanted to be a vet ever since he'd known her. Was she thinking of giving it all up because Doc had taken her mother in? He couldn't let her throw everything away like that.

"Why not?" he asked as he buckled up.

"Why not?" Mona repeated. She shoved the metal tongue on her seat belt into the slot. The click echoed within the vehicle. "Why not?" she said again, this time her voice swelling in volume.

"That's the question," Joe said, his tone level, nonthreatening. "Why wouldn't you go in to work tomorrow?"

"How can I go in there tomorrow and act as if nothing happened?" she asked incredulously. "It *did* happen. Doc lied to me, Joe. He *lied* to me. The man I trusted, looked up to, *believed* in, thought of as my father, for God's sake, lied to me. How could he do that? And how can I face him now? That woman was there, in his house, all along. She'd been there since the wedding."

Turning the key in the ignition, Joe put the Jeep into Drive and released the hand brake. "No, Doc didn't lie," he contradicted in the same emotionless voice.

Mona fisted her hands in her lap. "How can you say that?" she cried.

There was no moon out tonight. He turned on his high beams and picked his way back to the main road. The road that would take him to her house. "Did you ask him if your mother was staying with him?"

"No," she spat out, exasperated, "but—"

"Then he didn't lie." He glanced at her for a moment, then looked back on the road. "He just didn't tell you she was there."

"All right, then it's a sin of omission," she insisted, her voice breaking as she uttered the last word.

Damn it, she upbraided herself, she wasn't supposed to be this weak, this vulnerable. She was supposed to be able to say the hell with everything, everyone, keep her eyes front and just keep going, not fall apart this way like some delicate flower.

"Maybe," Joe allowed. He made a sharp right as they cleared the chapel. "Way I see it, he figured he'd get around to telling you once he felt you were ready to listen."

Mona stared straight ahead. Her reflection in the windshield bounced back at him. "Listen to what?"

"To your mother's side of it."

Mona could feel her resentment flaring all over

again. "She doesn't get to have a side. She dumped us and ran off to have fun."

"Maybe," Joe agreed, although he thought there might be more to it than that. Doc was a good man, but he wouldn't have taken the woman in if there wasn't more to Elena Ruiz's story. "But I doubt if she wound up having it."

"How the hell did you come to that conclusion?" she demanded.

"Because she's here, asking you to give her a chance. Because she didn't leave after you told her to go." He paused a moment, debating adding the next sentence, but if Mona was going to come around, she needed to know this. "Because she came back even after Rick told her to go that first time."

Mona stopped staring out the window and looked at him. What was he talking about? "What first time?"

"Your mother—"

"Elena," she corrected fiercely. The woman didn't deserve to be referred to as her mother.

"Elena," he amended for her sake, "was here before," he told her. "When you were around eighteen. She went to Rick to try to make things up to him and you. He told her that she was eighteen years too late and sent her away before you could see her. He didn't want you to be hurt," he added.

Just like she hadn't wanted Elena's return to spoil Rick's wedding day, Mona thought. She and Rick were protective of each other.

"Someone who keeps coming back like that," Joe was saying, "*really* wants to make amends."

"How do you know all this?" Mona asked. "That she came back before?"

"Elena told me when I escorted her out of Rick's wedding," Joe said. For a long moment after that Joe said nothing. But then he decided that he had to. Otherwise, by his silence, he would contribute to the mistake Mona was about to make and eventually, that mistake would haunt her. And when it did, it would be his fault.

"We only get one mother in our lifetime, Mona. Mine died when I was a kid and I would give anything, *anything,* just to be able to spend one more day with her. You're getting that chance. Don't turn your back on it."

Mona's expression hardened. "Your mother didn't abandon you. Didn't just leave you with the first person she thought of and then take off. Big difference," she insisted.

"No, not really," he contradicted. "Not to me at the time." She, of all people, should understand this, he thought, considering how she'd felt when her grandmother had died. "I felt as if she'd abandoned me and I was pretty mad at her for about two years. Maybe even longer." As he was passed from one indifferent distant relative to another, the resentment had been pretty intense at times. "Never mind that she hadn't wanted to die, bottom line to me was that she did. And she left me behind ten years old and scared, handed off from relative to relative like one of those cakes people try to get rid of at Christmas."

She supplied the name he couldn't remember automatically. "Fruit cake."

"That's the one." He could see her house in the distance and began to slow down. "Be the bigger person, Mona. Give Elena a chance to talk to you. If you don't like what she has to say, you haven't lost a thing. But if her apology is sincere, if you decide to forgive her for leaving in the first place, the way I see it, you're both getting a second chance."

She shook her head.

He knew that she could be the most stubborn person ever created and he understood that she was hurt, but he'd never known her to be unfair.

"Don't say no," Joe advised. "Say you'll think about it."

"I'm not saying no," she told him.

She'd been through a lot today. Maybe she was operating on the hairy edge. The corners of his mouth curved slightly. "You're supposed to nod your head, not shake it, if you're agreeing with me."

"I'm just stunned," Mona explained. He raised a quizzical eyebrow. "I don't think I've ever heard you say that many words at one time. Hell, I don't think I've ever heard you say that many words in a single day," she amended.

"It's the job," he commented, remembering that Alma and Larry had said almost the same thing the first day he was acting sheriff. "It makes you talk."

Hardly hearing him, Mona blew out a long breath, as if she was centering herself. "Okay," she finally agreed, "I'll let her talk to me." She raised her eyes to his. "I'll do it for you."

"No," Joe corrected her firmly. "You do it for *you*."

After pulling up in front of Mona's house, he put

the Jeep into Park and turned off the ignition. He still wasn't certain if she was actually all right. Moreover, her vulnerability affected him. It made him want to wrap her up in his arms and just protect her. From absolutely everything that gave her pain.

That would go over like the proverbial lead balloon if he so much as hinted at it. Still, he wanted Mona to know that she wasn't alone. That he was there for her if she needed him and he always would be.

"Want me to come in?" he asked quietly.

"Yes."

She said the word so quickly, it sounded as if it had come out riding on the end of his sentence. The moment he'd begun to ask, she realized just how much she wanted him to be with her. How much she didn't want to be alone tonight.

Her eyes met his and in what she hoped was a more sedate voice, Mona repeated the single word. "Yes." But even as she said it, it sounded more breathless than the first time.

Unbuckling, Joe got out of the vehicle on his side and came around to hers. By the time he reached her, Mona was already out, getting out her keys. She had the door unlocked and open just as Apache bounced out of the backseat. The dog ran between them, dashing into the house as if seeking shelter.

A lot of that going around tonight, Mona thought.

She walked in ahead of Joe. The moment he was inside and closed the door behind him, she turned around to face him. Everything inside of her was tingling. Set to go off.

He could feel the charge in the air, could feel his

capitulation shimmering despite all his noble intentions only to comfort her and then leave. He could feel his body wanting hers. Could feel the heat flaring between them.

If ever there was a need to lay ground rules, it was now.

"Mona—"

He got no further. She had captured his lips, rendering them useless. At least when it came to forming any intelligible words. They were pressed against hers, lost in a deep kiss. She literally took his breath away. Unable to resist, he wrapped his arms around her, held her close to him and kissed her with all the passion that he'd stored up over all these years.

Later he might tell himself that it was in self-defense but that would be a lie. Yes, she'd been the one to initiate this, but he was kissing her because he wanted to. He kissed her back with complete reckless abandon. Because what he was doing, what he was letting himself in for, *was* reckless. Acting on suppressed desires always was.

Up until this moment, he had been holding himself relatively in check. But the moment her lips had touched his, he couldn't do that any longer.

His reaction to her kiss wasn't born of the moment. It was, instead, the culmination of years of desire. If he'd thought that he'd outgrown it, the moment he'd seen her that first day, standing beside her car in the rain, it had overtaken him full force. All the time they'd spent together, everything they did together since then had only reinforced it.

Last week, he'd brought her to the reservation where

he had been born and his mother had been buried. Brought her there so he could show her, without words, what had shaped him. It was meant to be just a short trip but it hadn't turned out that way. They had wound up staying far into the night.

Several of the children on the reservation were down with a particularly strong strain of the flu. There was no doctor to treat them, no medicine available to them. It was all too costly and far away. So Mona had rolled up her sleeves, falling back on her initial basic medical training and done what she could. And he had been there, right by her side, lending support and aid.

It was an education in more ways than one. He learned that the antibiotic that she prescribed for ailing canines could also be given to ailing children.

"And I won't grow a tail or anything?" one of the little boys weakly asked her, even as a fever raged through his small, thin body. When she'd assured him that he wouldn't, he'd been crestfallen. And she had struggled not to laugh.

At that exact moment Joe was certain that he was in love with her. And just as certain that nothing would ever come of it.

But here they were, in her house, and she was kissing him. All of his noble resolve never to let her know how he felt, never to touch her like a lover, had just gone up in flames. Because if he *were* noble, he would gently but firmly break the connection.

Instead of embracing it. And her.

His blood rushed hot through his veins as his hands molded her to him, caressing her curves, caressing her. Each time his mouth left hers, it was only to return from another angle, kissing her over and over again, each time more deeply than the last.

He'd never felt like this, like some wild-eyed kid with his first girl. She made him feel that anything was possible. She made him feel reborn.

Reality, never far away, waited for him at first light. But right now, in this place, he could pretend that *this* was his reality, one that began and ended with her. With Mona.

A frenzy had descended over her. There was no other way to describe it. Mona felt as if she was on fire and she couldn't stop herself, not while the flames burned so brightly within her. She wasn't able to back away.

The more he kissed her, the more she wanted him to. She could feel the demands increasing inside her, ready to burst. Arching into him, she began to fumble at the buttons on his shirt, undressing him while her mouth was still sealed to his.

An eternity later, when all the buttons had finally been released, she pushed the shirt off Joe's shoulders and then struggled to get the sleeves off his arms. Progress was impeded by his rock-solid biceps.

Her breathing grew audible, each breath shorter than the last because the air in her lungs was rapidly being consumed in direct proportion to her increasing passion.

Time became a blur but everything was crystal clear to her. She was acutely aware of every pass of his hands, the feel of his warm breath along her skin. Aware of his hands as he slowly stripped her clothing away from her.

There were calluses on his fingers and palms. That

only intensified the delicious feel of them as his strong hands came in contact with her bare skin. It heated immediately in response to his touch, heated until she thought she would burn away to a small, black crisp.

She wanted him, wanted him to make love with her now, this instant. Wanted to be one with him before something happened and made the moment go away.

They tumbled onto the sofa, locked in an embrace, oblivious to everything else.

With each pass of his lips, the intensity within her gathered, making her ache for release even as she struggled to perpetuate the moment. She had never known she could feel this way, ecstatic and yet, in part, afraid. Afraid that, in the end, disappointment would be waiting for her. Disappointment just as there always had been in her life.

But if, at the last moment, she wanted to postpone the inevitable, she realized that she couldn't. The matter was completely out of her hands. Her body had taken command and, like a speeding train, it was hurrying to its culmination.

And around each bend, there was another surge, a surge that built upon the last and reached out to the next.

She arched and bucked, wanting to absorb it all while it lasted.

IT WAS JUST AS HE'D thought it would be. Only better. So incredibly better. This was where all his fantasies about her—when he allowed himself to have them—had promised to lead him.

There was just a micron of control left to him, a

slender thread that allowed him to, at the very end, go slower than he would have ordinarily wanted to. Go slower so that he could share with her and give her the same pleasure she gave him.

But he was only a man and in the end, even he had his limits.

His mouth sealed to hers, Joe moved his body until it was directly over her. With an agonizingly slow movement, he entered her, sealing their union. Holding fast to his resolve, Joe tried to move to a tempo that built up bit by bit, but that lasted less than a moment. Going slow was no longer an option.

They moved in harmony, faster and faster until he sensed she was almost at the final plateau just before the fireworks. Releasing himself, he joined her at the last second and as the atmosphere around them filled with the splendor of sky rockets bursting all around them, they shared the exquisite joy of reaching fulfillment together.

There was no denying it. He loved her.

Chapter Fourteen

Mona caught herself wanting to curl her body into his.

Now that the glorious shower of pleasure had subsided, she wanted to hold on to Joe, to enjoy the simple pleasure of feeling his warmth, feeling his body beside hers. Feeling him drawing breath next to her.

But that would be taking things for granted. That would be leaving herself wide open for disappointment, if not now, then soon. All too soon. She had learned a long time ago that you couldn't depend on people. Even people you gave your trust to.

And if that hadn't been driven home right from the beginning, or with the death of her grandmother, well, all she had to do was look to today. She would have sworn on a stack of bibles—if she was given to swearing—that she could trust Doc completely. That the man who'd been her mentor, who had funded her college education, would come through for her no matter what. That she could count on him to be there for her and to always, always be honest with her.

But in the end she couldn't rely on him. He had sided with the woman who had now decided to call herself her mother. God only knew why, but it had taught her a lesson. *No one* could be counted on if for some reason it went against their own interests.

So if she gave in to these feelings that she had for Joe, these feelings that he had skillfully aroused as sure as the sun would rise again tomorrow, she would crash and burn. Maybe not tomorrow, maybe not even the day after that, but crashing and burning would definitely happen and it would be sometime soon. Which meant that she would be left stricken again.

The only way around that was to brace herself for the inevitable. To rally by withdrawing into herself and to not expect *anything* from Joe.

Not even a replay of the physical experience that had just taken place.

For all she knew, she'd disappointed him. She wasn't exactly experienced. Joe, she had no doubt, had had a great many partners even though he didn't allude to them or bring up so much as one name. It was still something she was certain of, deep in her bones, and it made her worry that when measured against these nameless others, she came up short.

So, rather than curl up into him the way she longed to, Mona curled up into herself, assuming what amounted to an adult fetal position. It was not an easy trick within the confines of her sofa, which was barely wide enough to accommodate their two bodies, much less granting a separation between them.

Even so, Joe was aware of what she was doing. Aware that she was trying her damndest to pull away from him. Why?

He thought of pretending that he didn't notice.

Thought of getting up and getting dressed as if what had transpired between them was just part of a greater whole, but he liked lying here beside her. Liked the fact that, despite her efforts, their two bodies were still touching.

So he took the simplest route. He asked. "What's the matter?"

He felt her stiffening. "What makes you think there's something the matter?" Mona fired back.

"For one," he observed, "when you just answered me, you sounded like a machine gun going off in rapid succession. For another, you're pulling back into yourself like a bedsheet that's attempting to fold itself into a handkerchief."

Why was he always able to read her as if she was an open book? "Colorful," she said sarcastically. "Ever think of writing poetry?"

"No. Ever think of giving a straight answer?" Joe countered, his eyes on hers, pinning her down. He was tired of her blowing hot and cold whenever she was around him. The only thing worse would be *not* having her around him at all.

"I give straight answers all the time," Mona shot back indignantly.

"Maybe. To other people. But not to me, not this time," Joe pointed out quietly. "What's wrong, Mona?" he asked again, propping himself up on his elbow and looking down at her face. How many times had he dreamed of this moment? *Wished* for this moment? He couldn't allow it to end badly. "Did this scare you?" he wanted to know.

Digging into the sofa with her elbow, she rose up,

her face a couple of inches from his. "No!" Mona cried angrily.

Joe continued as if she hadn't said anything. "Because it sure as hell scared me," he admitted.

And it had. Because he'd felt things he wasn't supposed to. Things he'd never felt before. Longings that went beyond the moment. Longings, he knew, that were beyond his reach.

He was willing to enjoy the interlude. But he wasn't willing to get even more tangled up inside over someone who he ultimately hadn't a chance with, especially not when he was looking at forever.

He was certain that, if Mona thought of him at all, to her he was Joe-the-friend, or Joe-the-deputy, not Joe-possible-husband-material. Not in her world. In her world, she was completely out of his league. She'd never said it, but she didn't have to. His earlier life on the reservation, intentionally or not, had taught him what his ultimate place was. And that place wasn't with someone bright and fresh, witty and intelligent, like Mona.

Mona blinked. "You, scared?" she repeated in a mocking tone.

The Joe she knew wasn't threatened by anyone or anything. She didn't think that she'd even ever *heard* him use the word *scared* in reference to himself. Joe was *never* scared. It was one of the givens of life. He was different than the rest of them. And that difference had always made him special to her, even though she would never admit it to him.

"Why would you be scared?" she questioned.

His eyes held hers for a long moment, hypnotizing her. Hypnotizing himself.

Joe swept back the hair from her face, cupping her cheek gently. "You ask too many questions, woman," he murmured just before he kissed her.

The questions remained, but for the time being, they faded away, replaced by the fiery sensation that once again leaped to the foreground the moment his lips touched hers.

He wanted her. That was all she needed to know right now.

MONA LONGED TO REMAIN in that nice warm cocoon that they had woven together in the night, but morning arrived with its own ideas.

She wasn't the type to run away from problems, even though a large part of her wanted to. If she did, setting a precedent, the very action would make her disgusted with herself. She prided herself on the fact that she wasn't a quitter, that she didn't run. She was a fighter. And somehow, although she wasn't sure as to the exact logistics that had been involved, Joe had convinced her to hear her mother out and allow her to make amends.

So, Mona showered and got dressed—actions that took her longer than usual, given that she was doing neither alone—and had Joe drive her and Apache back to the cemetery so that she could retrieve her vehicle.

From there, she would to drive to Doc's. Without Joe.

"You sure you're going to be all right?" Joe asked,

unaware that he was allowing his concern about her show through so strongly.

He was worried about her, she thought. That gave her the exact push to see this through. It was the reverse of a dare, but it had the exact same effect.

"Of course I'm going to be all right," she told him with feeling comprised mostly of sheer bravado. "I'm always all right."

"If you say so." She couldn't tell by his tone if he was mocking her or being doubtful.

Or just being Joe and thus completely unreadable.

In any case, she needed to get going before her courage deserted her. Mona patted the seat beside her in the Jeep. The next moment, Apache leaped into the vehicle. She leaned over to close the passenger side door.

Time to see this through and make everyone else happy, she thought, lumping Joe and Doc into the same group.

They both drove into town with Joe turning right and going on to the sheriff's office, while she turned left and drove to the animal clinic.

Doc was already there when she walked in. He was doing something at the receptionist's desk and looked up when the door opened.

"Mona." Relief washed over his broad face only to give way to a look of uncertainty and concern. "I didn't know if you were going to come in today."

"Why wouldn't I come in?" she asked, forcing her voice to sound cheerful. "Delia Morales is bringing in her cat to be declawed today. I made the appointment for her myself. Wouldn't exactly look right if I didn't show up and the cat did. I'm guessing that your agenda's full today."

He nodded, but it was obvious that his mind wasn't on the day's appointments. He trod lightly.

"Mona, about yesterday, I'm sorry. I should have told you that she—" he prudently refrained from referring to his houseguest as her mother "—was staying with me. Elena and I go way back," he told her. "Back to even before she married your father. She wasn't exactly what you might call disciplined. Unharnessed energy was the way I used to think of her."

He appeared to be unaware of the fond expression that slid over his face. But Mona wasn't. She refused to allow her thoughts to go any further and explore the reason for his look. There was only so much she could handle at one time.

"You should have seen her back then," Doc was saying, "before she was even your age. She was the most beautiful sight God ever created."

Mona listened to him, to the man she had always had such respect for, such affection, and despite her attempts to block the thought, she realized that he wasn't just giving shelter to a distraught soul, he was doing it because he'd had feelings for the woman. Feelings for Elena. Strong feelings.

He still did, her mind whispered.

She didn't know if that made her feel angrier—or feel happy for Doc, who, as far as she knew, never had anyone in his life to care about in that way.

"I'd take it as a personal favor if you heard her out, Mona," Doc appealed to her. "She really wants another chance to be the mother she couldn't be before. I know that in your eyes she's done nothing to deserve another chance, but—"

"Are you in love with Elena?" Mona asked abruptly.

The unexpected question appeared to jar him for a moment. She knew she'd never spoken to him like that, but then, he'd never hurt her like this before, never taken someone else's side against her before.

"What I feel for her doesn't matter," Doc replied in his quiet, even voice. "What does matter is your relationship with her—or lack of one. Some day, Mona, she won't be around. I don't want you to look back then and realize that you're feeling guilty about your behavior toward—"

"What makes you think I'll feel guilty?" she asked. For the moment, she decided not to tell him that Joe had already driven home the point he now tried to make.

Doc paused for a moment, as if wrestling with an issue. When he began to talk, he told her something about himself he'd never shared with anyone. "Because I had an absentee father and had the same feelings about him as you do about your mother. And when he came back into my life suddenly some twenty years later, I didn't want to have anything to do with him."

She could see by his expression that this was hard for Doc to talk about. Doc, who had always been able to talk about anything without hesitation. She realized that by telling her this, he tried to spare her the same kind of guilt.

"He left," Doc was saying, "and I never saw him again. I didn't know at the time that he was dying and he'd wanted to make amends so that he could die in peace."

Doc paused, taking a long breath. "I didn't give him that peace and sometimes, when I sit back and take stock of my life, that comes up to haunt me." His eyes peered into hers. "It's on the minus side of the tally."

She wanted to put her arms around him, around the young man he'd been, feeling abandoned just as she had. "How old were you when he left?"

Doc shrugged, the white lab coat he wore moving about his wide, powerful shoulders. "Six, seven, I don't remember exactly. What I do remember was the look on his face the last time I saw him. He was anguished and heartbroken. And I had done that to him, to another human being. To my father." His voice was kind, supplicating. "I don't want you to feel the same way, Mona."

It suddenly occurred to her that maybe Doc was trying to tell her something covertly. She felt a chill go zigzagging along her spine. "Are you telling me that she's dying, Doc?"

Her question seemed to throw him for a second. "What?" He then realized she might have picked that up from his own story. "No, but that doesn't change anything. If you send her away, you'll carry that look in her eyes around with you for the rest of your life." He took her hands into his. "I don't want that for you."

Mona blew out a breath. She loved Doc and didn't like these mixed emotions. In her heart, she *knew* that he was only thinking of her. But a part of her still resisted what he asked her to do. Resisted and nursed hurt feelings.

If she was honest with herself, she knew that Doc and Joe were both right in their urgings. It wasn't her nature to harbor a grudge. Bearing one against her mother was like a dark force that ate away at her soul and she'd kept it inside of her for a long time now. Long enough.

With a nod of her head, Mona gave in. "Is she still upstairs?"

"Yes," he told her. "Upstairs and packing."

Packing. Elena was leaving. That meant that all she had to do was keep busy and out of the way. By the end of the day, her problem would be gone and life would go back to the way she knew it.

Kind of, she amended, thinking of last night and Joe. After experiencing that, nothing would ever really be the same again. There was another factor to consider. She was now a sister-in-law, as well as a sister. That changed a lot.

It wasn't just Rick and her against the world anymore. Their family was expanding. Within a couple of months, she'd be an aunt. And Rick would be a father. She supposed that it would be a good thing for the baby to have a grandmother, and Olivia's parents were both dead.

Mona made up her mind.

"I'm going to take a break, Doc," Mona informed the senior veterinarian.

Without waiting for Doc to comment on the fact that she hadn't begun to work yet, she went toward the rear of the clinic and went to the back stairs. Gripping the handrail, she made her way slowly up to the second floor and Doc's living quarters.

When she came to the landing, she stood there for a second, waiting for her heart to settle down again. It had gone into double time as she tried to anticipate the words that would pass between her and her mother.

She hadn't a clue.

Taking another breath, she made her way to the last bedroom. The room she had found her mother the previous time. The bedroom door stood ajar. Rather than push it open, she knocked on it lightly and waited.

"Come in, Henry," she heard her mother respond. "I'm almost finished."

Mona opened the door and stepped over the threshold. Her mother's back was to the doorway. She was bent over an opened suitcase that was on the bed, trying to arrange what went inside.

"I'm not even good at packing," she said, still thinking she was talking to Doc. "I can't seem to get everything back into the suitcase. It all fit when I came," Elena lamented, shaking her head. "Don't see why it won't go back in now."

"You're leaving." It was a question hidden in the guise of a statement.

She saw her mother stiffen, then turn around, a look of tentative disbelief on her face, as if she thought her ears were playing tricks on her. When she saw who was in her bedroom, the look of stunned surprise froze for a moment on her face.

"Yes," Elena finally answered, "I'm leaving." She took a breath, as if to steady her voice, which trembled. "I thought it would be better that way. Whether you believe me or not, I don't want to cause you and your brother any more pain than I already have, and it seems that having me around does that, so I'm leaving."

Mona took another step closer to her mother. "Where will you go?"

The shrug was careless. And hapless. "I don't know yet." The smile that came to Elena's lips seemed forced. "It's a big country and there are a lot of places I haven't seen yet."

"They'll still be there later," Mona told her quietly, seriously. "I mean, if you don't go now."

Elena looked at her uncertainly. The question she asked was uttered very carefully, as if she was afraid of hearing the answer. Of being wrong. "Are you asking me to stay?"

"Well, if you go," Mona told her, "then neither one of us will ever know if this has a chance in hell of working, will we?"

Her mother's deep brown eyes were searching hers. "Are you saying that you forgive me?" Her voice rose at the end of the question as joy and hope wove their way through it.

Mona couldn't jump into it that fast, even though a small kernel inside of her wanted to. The small part that belonged to the little girl who had lain in bed, night after night, wondering what it would be like to have a mother who loved her.

"No, I'm not saying that. I'm saying that I'm leaving myself open to the possibility of forgiving you. If I feel that you deserve it," Mona qualified. "Doc seems to think you do and Joe thinks I should give you a second chance and I've always had a lot of respect for both their opinions." Pausing because she was afraid her voice would break, Mona pressed her lips together before going on. "So, I suppose what I'm saying is that

I'm willing to give this relationship a try—if you're really serious about making amends."

"Oh, I'm serious," Elena said quickly, tears gathering in her eyes only to come spilling down her cheeks. "I'm very serious," she assured Mona with enough feeling to fill a stadium. There was silence for a moment, and then Elena said, "I need you to know that leaving you and your brother here with your grandmother was the best thing I could have done for either of you. I wasn't stable. After your father died, I couldn't take care of you, either of you. I wasn't a fit mother. I wasn't even a fit person."

"You don't have to explain right now."

"Oh, but I do. It took me a long time to forgive myself. Forgive myself for being alive when your father was dead. By the time I worked things through, years had gone by. I didn't know how to come back. And when I finally did, Enri—Rick sent me away. It took me eight more years to work up the nerve to try again."

"I won't send you away this time," Mona told Elena quietly.

Elena steepled her fingers together before her lips to keep the sobs from escaping. And then, in a shaking voice she struggled to keep even, she had to ask, "Am I allowed to hug you?"

Mona said nothing. Instead, she silently held out her arms. Elena fell into them, sobbing loudly.

Mona struggled valiantly not to do the same. In the end, she lost.

Chapter Fifteen

"Your brother's coming back tomorrow."

Joe's quiet voice broke through the echoes of subsiding euphoria within her bedroom.

They were lying together in her bed, the way they had been every night since that first time. This was a new frontier he'd crossed. The women he'd bedded before had one thing in common. He rarely saw them twice, certainly not more than a handful of times. This was entirely different. Different and amazingly satisfying, although he tried not to explore as to why. He knew the danger in that. Mona would bolt.

He had his arm tucked around her, keeping Mona close to him. He knew all this was temporary, the way someone reluctant to wake up from a good dream knew without being told that it couldn't last forever. Dreams never did.

"I know," she murmured, loving the way her body curled into Joe's. Lying beside him like this was almost her favorite part of their lovemaking. The operative word being *almost*.

Funny how her perspective on things had changed in such an incredibly short amount of time. When her brother left with Olivia for their honeymoon, she'd felt gnawingly alone again, like someone forced to remain on the train platform while her life pulled away, locked tightly inside the train that was departing from the station.

And now, now things were different. So very different.

Mona turned into Joe, tilting her head so she could look up at him. "I wonder what's going to surprise Rick more, that I'm actually talking to our mother or that you and I are…"

Her voice trailed off as she realized she didn't know what to call what she and Joe were now. Lovers? That was too solid a word. She was going to say "together" but that might scare him away, as well, and besides, he'd never actually come out and said anything to make her believe that this was more than a pleasant interlude for him.

"Are more than friends," Mona finally said for lack of another, better term to describe where their relationship had now gone.

And even that, she thought, looking at Joe's impassive face, seemed not to be the right thing to say. So what *were* they? What did he think their togetherness meant?

She waited for him to speak, to jump in and tell her what he was feeling.

"You're going to tell Rick about…this?" Joe questioned.

He was being deliberately vague because Mona appeared to have gone out of her way *not* to label what was going on between them. He especially avoided the word *relationship* because he knew how Mona didn't trust relationships.

"No," she replied, sensing that that was the answer Joe was after. "I'm not going to go out of my way to specifically mention it. Why?" At the last moment, she'd decided to confront him. This playing games couldn't continue indefinitely. Either he was committed or he wasn't. And if he wasn't, she needed to know now, not six months down the road after she'd irretrievably lost her heart. "You don't want my brother to know you're…'seeing' me?"

God, but it was hard second-guessing what she wanted to hear. He went with a traditional excuse, even though, as far as he was concerned, it carried no weight with him. If he believed that Mona actually cared about him, about them, he would go up against Rick in a heartbeat.

As he spoke, Joe watched her face for a reaction. "Rick's my boss. Bosses usually don't like their employees sleeping with their sisters. Besides, you said this was no big thing."

She'd said that for his benefit—and, she supposed in part to keep from scaring herself. It was, she knew deep in her heart, a lie right from the very beginning. This was a *very* big deal. At least, it was to her.

But obviously not to Joe.

"Right," she said, keeping her tone matter-of-fact to hide the hurt all but exploding inside her. "It isn't. No big deal at all." She sat up, holding the sheet to her. She wanted him gone—before he could see her cry. "Look, since Rick and Olivia are coming back tomorrow, maybe I should clean up a little bit." She kept her face averted, avoiding his eyes. "Would you mind letting yourself out?"

The cool tone jarred him, but then, maybe that was what he needed, he told himself. Something to shove him out of the fool's paradise he'd constructed for himself. He'd foolishly created it despite all his self-imposed warnings that she was out of his reach. He'd known from the beginning that giving in to his feelings would make retreating back to his life that much harder.

It was coming to an end a lot faster than he'd thought, but then, it served him right for letting his guard down.

"Sure thing," Joe said. Sitting up, he grabbed his jeans from the floor and slid into them. He put on his shirt just as quickly.

Sure thing, her mind echoed bitterly. No objection, no "Why so quick?" No protest on his part. If she really listened closely, she might even be able to detect relief in his voice. Relief because now he didn't have to go through some kind of a scene as he broke it off with her, she thought angrily. He had his fun and now he was going to be free.

And she had fallen in love with him.

How could she have been so stupid?

Just because her mother finally returned didn't mean that the pattern that had haunted her life for so long was broken. One way or another, she was still the one who got left behind, physically or emotionally. By everyone who mattered.

Mona felt the bed shifting. Joe was on his feet. "See you around," she heard Joe say to her back.

Mona didn't bother to turn around, didn't suddenly jump up, the sheet wrapped around her, and implore him to stay. She didn't even answer his parting line with some kind of banal response. She just wanted him gone. Now. Before she *did* do something stupid. Like beg him to stay, to make love with her and make her feel that the magical moment would last forever.

And when, less than a couple of minutes later, she heard the front door close, she let out the shaky breath she'd been holding. But instead of getting up to clean the way she'd told him she intended to, Mona fell back on the bed, curled up and cried what was left of her jagged, scarred heart out.

UNABLE TO SLEEP, HER body almost bruised from all the tossing and turning she'd done, Mona finally got up a little after one in the morning. It was then that she finally turned her attention to cleaning the house. She judged that maybe, if she was busy enough, the pain would fade for a little while and leave her in peace.

And maybe, your next trip out of Forever will be to Oz, she silently mocked herself.

Feeling dead inside, she got busy.

MONA LOST TRACK OF TIME.

All that mattered was cleaning, cleaning everything within an inch of its life. She kept up a steady stream of conversation, talking to Apache as if the dog was diligently absorbing every word she said. Several times during her cleaning frenzy, Apache came up to her and licked her hand, but not as if fishing for treats. She could have sworn she saw a look of empathy in the soft brown eyes as the animal looked up her.

He knew, she thought. Knew her heart was breaking. Animals could be eerily intuitive at times.

"Too bad the guy who brought you to me doesn't have some of your skills," she said out loud.

It was time to stop feeling sorry for herself and start making plans for the rest of her life. If Doc felt as if he had the situation under control, she might see about setting up a practice in Dallas the way Rick had suggested when she'd returned.

She paused, one window shy of finishing her task, letting the sponge fall into the dirty water in the bucket.

"What do you think, Apache? Would you like to go live in Dallas?"

The dog didn't bark. Instead, cocking his head he just looked at her, his eyes mirroring the deadness in her soul.

The dog definitely had more on the ball than Joe did. She sank her hands into the bucket again, squeezing the sponge, ready to keep going until the house sparkled and she dropped from exhaustion. Hopefully the two wouldn't be mutually exclusive.

"YOU'RE WHAT?" LARRY echoed, looking at Joe as if the latter had just lost his mind.

Joe took a breath. After the way things had ended last night, he knew he couldn't remain in Forever. The town was too small for him not to keep running into Mona. Seeing her and not *being* with her would just be too painful for him. He had to leave. As soon as possible.

He'd decided to break the news to Larry first in preparation for telling Rick. So far, this wasn't the reception he'd anticipated.

"I'm thinking of trying my luck some place else," he repeated in the same monotone voice he'd used to tell Larry in the first place. Anything else and he was afraid he'd give his feelings away.

"Like as in leaving Forever?" Larry asked incredulously.

"Like as in leaving Forever," Joe confirmed with a quick nod of his head.

Larry frowned and shook his head. "You and Mona had a fight, didn't you?"

Joe maintained his stoic look. "No, no fight."

Larry moved so that he was directly in front of him, leaving only inches between their faces. "Then what?"

"Then," Joe continued in the same emotionless voice, "this is none of your business."

Beneath Larry's perpetually tanned face hints of red brought on by frustrated anger appeared. "It is if it means suddenly having the team cut down by a quarter. If you two *did* have a fight, just go say you're sorry. Women love to hear that."

Larry had been unattached for as long as Joe had known him. "And you'd be the expert on what women want, right?"

Larry looked as if he was about to defend himself, but then he switched directions. "We're not talking about me, we're talking about you. If we were talking about me," he couldn't resist tacking on, "you'd know that I don't brag about my interactions with the fairer sex." The blond deputy reverted back to the main topic. "Now, whatever it is that's going on between the two of you, it can be fixed. You just have to—"

"There's nothing going on," Joe denied. "And nothing to fix." He drew a fortifying breath. "I just realized that I was right."

Larry shrugged carelessly. "First time for everything." He pinned his friend with a look, waiting. "What is it you were right about?"

Ordinarily, Joe kept his own counsel. But Larry was his friend. If this was one of the last conversations they had, he might as well let the deputy know and appease his vociferous curiosity.

"That Mona's out of my league." He tossed Larry a bone. "It was fun while it lasted, but now it's time to get back to reality."

Larry eyed him, clearly annoyed at his reasoning. "And reality's in another town?"

Joe shrugged. "Maybe. Because it sure isn't here."

"You're making a big mistake."

"No," Joe contradicted, "I already made one and now I'm trying to move on." He was done explaining himself. Joe crossed back to his desk. "Now, leave me alone for a while. I've got a resignation letter to put together."

RICK SENSED SOMETHING was wrong the minute he saw his sister. Despite the fact that Mona threw her arms around both him and Olivia when they stepped out of the hired car, the forced smile on her lips didn't sit right with him.

He was even further convinced that he was right when, several minutes later, as he shut the front door behind them, Mona suddenly told them that she intended to take his advice and go back to Dallas. She planned to set up an animal hospital there.

His own advice was coming back to bite him, Rick thought, looking at Mona. When he realized that she wasn't even faintly excited about the prospect she'd just outlined, he decided to try to get at the real reason for this sudden change of heart.

"Just like that?" he asked. "Five weeks ago, you didn't want to hear about it when I tried to talk to you about it."

"What can I say? I bow to your wisdom," Mona said flippantly, then flashed a grin at her sister-in-law. "He'll make you crazy being right," she confided.

"I already know that," Olivia laughed, her hand resting protectively on her abdomen and the swell created by their unborn child.

"Besides," Mona continued, quickly glancing at Rick, then away in case he saw the doubt in her eyes. "A girl's got to think of her future."

He exchanged looks with the woman who'd won his heart. Olivia appeared as mystified as he was. "Exactly what happened to change your mind?" Rick asked, trying to pin his sister down.

"Nothing," Mona insisted stubbornly. "Like I said, I just decided that you were right. There's no future for me here."

Mona's acknowledgment that he was right just

aroused his suspicions further. Mona *never* admitted that he was right—about *anything.* She lived to argue and loved a good verbal sparring match more than anyone he knew. He needed to get to the bottom of this and it wasn't going to be by asking Mona. First chance he got, he would talk to Miss Joan.

BUT TIME WAS IN SCARCE supply that first day. He and Olivia had only begun to unpack when Doc dropped by to tell them that he was holding a welcome home party for them that evening. With a twinkle in his eye, the vet told them that he wasn't about to take no for an answer.

The party would be as good a place as any, Rick thought, to corner Miss Joan.

But it was Doc who cornered him first, as well as Olivia, at the party. Acting more mysterious than Rick could remember the older man ever behaving, Doc took them both aside and informed them that, "Your mother's in town, Rick, and she wants to meet with you and your lovely bride here."

Rick felt Olivia's hand tighten comfortingly on his arm. But he wasn't thinking about himself. This could be the reason for Mona's sudden decision to leave. If it was, he wouldn't allow it. Mona meant a lot more to him than an absentee mother.

"Does Mona know?" he asked Doc.

Doc nodded, his blue eyes crinkling kindly. "Mona knows."

He was right, Rick thought. "And?" he pressed, wanting to hear further details so he could decide whether or not he was actually right.

Doc smiled. "She's coming around. It took her a bit, but I think Joe convinced her."

"Joe?" Rick repeated uncertainly. "What does Joe have to do with it?"

"Everything." The smile had turned into a grin. A large, amused grin that instantly traveled up to Doc's eyes and took over his whole countenance. "A lot of things've been happening since you two went on your honeymoon."

"Things," Rick echoed. "What kind of things?" Then, before Doc could answer, he had another question for the man. "Did Mona tell you that she wants to leave Forever?"

Doc nodded. "For Dallas. Yes, Mona told me this morning. If you ask me, her leaving has something to do with Joe leaving."

Rick stared at Doc in disbelief. He hadn't been to the office yet and this was the first he'd heard about his deputy's sudden plans. He would have bet that Joe intended to stay in Forever, well, forever.

Confused, Rick held his hand up to stop Doc. "Hold it. Now Joe's leaving? Since when?"

"Since today, from what I hear. Miss Joan saw him this morning. First time he'd stopped by for breakfast in a couple of weeks according to her," he added subtly. "She said Joe seemed pretty set on going."

Rick sighed. In the short time they'd been gone, all hell had broken loose.

He looked at Olivia. "That does it. I'm putting you on notice. We're not going on another honeymoon. Too much happens when we're away."

Olivia smiled. "That's okay with me," she said, then

whispered in his ear. "We can create our own honey-moon wherever we are."

Rick felt his heart swelling and thought for the umpteenth time that he was one lucky man. He hadn't realized this kind of happiness existed until Olivia had come into his life.

"Now, what are you going to do about Mona and Joe?" she wanted to know, asking the question loud enough for Doc to hear, too.

As much as he didn't want either one of them to leave, Rick didn't think there was anything he actually *could* do. Considering how independent Olivia was, he was surprised that she'd even ask.

"Nothing. They're both adults. I can't tell them what to do. They can make their own decisions."

The answer didn't please Olivia. She leaned her head into his.

"Look at them," she insisted, first indicating Mona, who was walking away from Miss Joan, and then Joe, who was apparently doing the same thing as he put distance between himself and Larry. "They look mis-erable," Olivia pointed out—as if she needed to. "As miserable as you and I were when I went back to Dallas and you stayed here," she reminded him.

He had to agree that neither his sister nor his senior deputy seemed very happy. On the contrary, they both appeared angry and annoyed. He had a hunch Miss Joan and Larry had urged each to stay in Forever and give love another chance.

He knew his sister well enough to know that she instantly chaffed whenever someone told her what to do. When she was a little girl, she would always do the exact opposite just to show that she was master of her own destiny. It led to a lot of clashes with Abuela.

And as for Joe, the deputy was far more laid-back than Mona, but the man had worked for him for five years. Long enough for him to discover that in his own way, the full-blood Apache was every bit as stubborn as his sister. He displayed his mindset more quietly, but the "destination" was the same.

A union between these two would be pretty damn interesting, Rick mused. Not to mention fiery.

Olivia was right. He had to keep Mona and Joe from going off to the opposite ends of the earth and find a way to get them back together again. And make them think it was their own idea. That part was crucial.

That would also be the tricky part.

"Enrique?"

About to attempt to approach Mona, Rick stopped dead when he heard the woman's low voice coming from behind him. Only one person ever called him that.

Turning around, he found himself looking into the face of the woman whose features he had tried so often to erase from his mind.

He realized that he didn't feel that same urgency anymore. He was married now, and somehow that state had expanded his range, made him see things that he'd been oblivious to before. Made the concept of family that much more important.

The woman watching him anxiously looked thinner than he remembered. Also smaller in stature somehow. But she still had the flowing midnight-black hair, pinned back now. Hair that he and Mona shared. She also didn't seem nearly as confident as he recalled.

"I don't want to bother you," she said hesitantly. "I just wanted to say hello." Wetting her lips, her eyes darted fleetingly to Olivia and then back to him. She looked as if she was ready to retreat quickly if he rejected her. "I can leave if you—"

He didn't let her finish. He didn't want her to leave. The time for retaliation, for revenge and giving back as good as he felt he'd received, was behind him. So instead, he slipped his hand around the back of Olivia's widening waist and said, "Olivia, I'd like you to meet my mother, Elena Ruiz."

Rick couldn't recall ever seeing anyone's smile as wide as the one gracing the woman his wife was meeting for the first time. It warmed his heart.

Chapter Sixteen

"Hi, Mona, how's it going?" Larry asked brightly when she reluctantly walked into the sheriff's office the next morning.

"Lousy," Mona replied, saying the first thing that came to her mind. It aptly described the way she felt.

She didn't want to be here where she could easily run into Joe. But when her brother had called her less than half an hour ago, Rick had insisted that it was pretty much a matter of life or death that she get herself over to his office immediately.

Ordinarily, she'd balk at having her brother order her to make an appearance, but the tone of his voice made her feel that something was wrong, something he assured her he couldn't discuss over the phone. For leverage, he reminded her that within a matter of days, she'd be gone and they wouldn't see one another for who knew how long.

Guilt was always a sharp, handy tool because it worked.

"Sorry to hear that," Larry commented on her reply. He seemed sincere. "Sorry, too, to hear that you'll be leaving us again so soon. Sure you want to go? You've only been back a little over a month," he said as if she wasn't aware of how long it had been since her arrival.

"Rick told you I was leaving?" Mona asked, thoroughly surprised. Her brother had never been one of those talkative types who shared family business. But then, maybe her new sister-in-law had an effect on him, changing him for the better. Still, she would have preferred if she hadn't been the topic he'd used to wet his feet after his transformation.

Mona looked around, but Rick wasn't in the outer room. Maybe he'd changed his mind about this life-or-death emergency after all. "Is my brother around?" she asked Larry.

"Yes, that he is," Larry told her with fanfare she found rather odd. "He said, when you got here, I should bring you right into his office."

As he spoke, Larry took her arm, slipping it through his as if they were going on a long stroll and he was to be her guide.

"I know where the office is, Larry," she told him. But as she tried to reclaim her arm by slipping it out again, she found that Larry had tightened his hold on her. Just what was going on here?

"I know you know, but the sheriff was very clear. He told me to bring you right in, not 'send' you right in, so I'm doing just that. I'm bringing you in," he declared with an easygoing grin. As if sensing her resistance, he explained. "Man signs my paychecks, I try to follow his instructions down to the letter. No sense in giving him an excuse to fire me. Times are tough," he concluded with a deep sigh.

Larry was acting strange, she thought, even for Larry. She glanced around, hoping to spot Alma and appeal to her. But the female deputy was nowhere around.

They'd just reached Rick's tiny inner office. Because of the glass enclosure, she could see right in. Rick wasn't alone.

Mona dug her feet in and stopped moving.

"He's got Joe in there," she protested.

Larry did a double take and appeared properly surprised. No one's acting career would ever be threatened by Larry, she thought darkly.

"Why, I do believe you're right. But he's just finishing up, so you can go on in," Larry coaxed, tugging on her arm to get her to cross the last few feet. He opened the door to the sheriff's office and announced, "Brought her right in just like you wanted, Sheriff."

Mona absolutely refused to budge. With a mumbled, "Sorry," Larry placed the flat of his hand against her back and gave her just enough of a push to get her across the threshold.

The moment she was in, he quickly closed the door behind her.

For a split second, as she was being propelled into the room, she noticed that Joe looked as surprised as she did that they were in the small enclosed space together.

Rick had called him in five minutes ago to ask why he was so hell-bent on leaving Forever after all this time. And so suddenly, too.

"No reason," Joe had answered, determined not to say anything about getting together with Mona while the sheriff was on his honeymoon. The less Rick knew about that, the better. He didn't believe in completely burning his bridges behind him. "Just thought it was time for me to move on."

"Got a job lined up?" Rick had asked, giving him one of his penetrating looks.

Joe knew that it would be better all around if he just pretended that he had landed a job in another town. He debated even saying that he'd been offered a position as a state trooper.

But being Joe, lies did not rest easily on his tongue, so what he'd wound up saying was, "Something's in the works," letting it go at that. It was sufficiently vague to assuage his conscience and yet sounded viable. There was no reason for Rick to know the truth.

He'd just mumbled his answer when the door to Rick's office had opened and Larry had all but shoved Mona in. She'd stopped a couple of inches away from him.

For once, he managed to recover before Mona did. "Well, I see you're going to be busy, Sheriff, so I'll just go—"

Rick rounded his desk and presented his body before the door, guarding it with his back. "No, you won't," he cut his deputy off sternly.

"All right, then I'll go," Mona informed him haughtily. She was nothing if not angry at being ambushed like this. It just proved that she really *couldn't* trust Rick anymore.

"Stay!" Rick ordered, freezing her in her tracks.

Mona turned from the door, anger flaring in her eyes like twin green flames. Just who the hell did he think he was?

"I'm not a dog, Rick," she said between clenched teeth.

"Damn straight you're not," Rick fired back. "Dogs are a hell of a lot more obedient." His stern gaze swept over Joe, as well as his sister. "Look, I just have something to say to both of you and then you can go running off your separate ways," he tagged on in barely controlled disdain. "I figure after all this time, I've earned five minutes from each of you."

Mona glared at her brother, hating that he was making her feel this awkward, this uncomfortable. "Get on with it," she snapped, far from happy about having to listen to anything while standing so close to Joe.

"Go ahead, Sheriff," Joe said in a far more genial voice. "I'm listening."

There wasn't even the slightest hint of a smile on Rick's face, nothing to give away the true nature of his thoughts. "I just wanted to tell you that I think both of you are doing the right thing, leaving Forever."

"What?" Mona asked, stunned.

She'd expected just the opposite from Rick after the scene last night. Despite the fact that he'd been the one to try to convince her to pursue her future in the big city, he'd been very upset when she'd told him that she'd made up her mind to leave Forever as soon as possible.

"You heard me," Rick said, the first glimmer of a smile surfacing. "I thought it over and it's the best thing. I mean, whatever it is you two thought you had together, well, that's clearly not going to work out," he pronounced with a laugh. "If you think you're in love, you're just deluding yourselves. I never met two people who were so wrong for each other.

"She'll drive you crazy in less than six months," he told Joe, "and you'll wind up strangling her just to get some peace and quiet and I'll have to arrest you. Trust me. I'll miss you both, but I for one am really glad you came to your senses before it was too late." He looked from one to the other, as if assuring himself that his words had sank in. "Okay, that's all." He moved back behind his desk again and sat down, ready to get to work. "You can go now," he said, gesturing for them both to leave.

If he thought she could be dismissed like some errant schoolgirl, Rick was sadly mistaken, Mona thought, working herself up.

"I'm not going anywhere," Mona declared angrily, her hands on her hips as she glared at her brother. "And no, that's not 'all.' Not by a long shot. Who the hell do you think you are, making assumptions like that about me? About Joe and me?" she wanted to know.

Palms spread out on his desk, she leaned into her brother's face. "I can love anyone I choose—without your damn approval. And if I want to be with Joe, or not be with Joe, that's *my* choice to make, not yours, understand?" she demanded. Not waiting for an answer, she continued. "And if I want to marry Joe, then I'll marry Joe and while it would be nice to have you happy about it, contrary to anything you might think, I don't need your blessings, Big Brother. Understand?"

He took so long to answer, Mona thought her brother hadn't heard her. Just as she was about to repeat her words, he said, "But you're just talking hypothetically, right?" Rick asked, slanting a look toward Joe as he addressed his words to his sister. Joe, he knew, needed to have a fire lit beneath him.

"No, I'm not talking hypothetically. Does this look like I'm being hypothetical?" she snapped. Spinning around on her heel, she grabbed hold of the front of Joe's shirt for leverage and raised herself up on her toes. The next second she was pressing her lips against Joe's, delivering a kiss that was more fire than passion.

The passion showed up a split second later, like a giant wave breaking over her head, soaking all of her and taking her breath away.

She'd gotten caught in her own trap.

Mona stumbled back, realizing belatedly what she'd just done—and with her brother looking on, too.

What the hell was she thinking?

Thoroughly stunned, Joe only allowed her to take a single step back. His arms had closed around her in an instant, holding Mona in place before she could run. He'd anticipated her flight because she had that look in her eyes, the look that told him she was about to take off as if that would somehow negate what she'd just done in an unguarded moment.

Not by a long shot, he thought.

"Did you mean what you just said?" Joe asked.

Stalling, realizing that in her flash of temper, she'd said far too much, *done* far too much, Mona asked, "What part?"

"All of it," Joe said with emphasis, and then his voice softened. "Especially the part where you said you'd marry me."

Okay, she was in too deep to backpedal. She tossed

her head. "If I wanted to. I said I'd marry you if I wanted to," she reminded him, as if that somehow covered up what she was really feeling for him—that Joe was the other part of her soul.

Not this time, Joe thought.

He wasn't about to let Mona worm her way out of this with fancy rhetoric and fancier footwork. As for him, maybe leaving quietly wasn't the way to go just yet. Since Rick had forced this face-to-face confrontation on them, he either had to fish or cut bait.

He didn't want to cut bait. He would ask her for a direct answer. If Mona told him that she didn't love him, then he *would* leave town and never bother her again. But right now, he needed that shove to get him out the door. Because leaving silently would just be the coward's way and he wasn't a coward.

"And do you want to marry me?" he asked pointedly, his eyes pinning her down, holding her to the truth.

Mona felt antsy inside. She didn't want to go first, didn't want to admit that she loved him if he kept his emotions a secret.

"You haven't asked me," she challenged.

He hadn't asked because he wasn't getting the feedback from her that would have encouraged him to take that final leap over the abyss. He'd had enough pain in his life, he didn't want to willingly subject himself to more.

But imagining the rest of his life without Mona amounted to the greatest pain of all. He didn't want that kind of life, filled with nothing but routines and emptiness. He'd already experienced that for far too long.

It was time to ante up and bet everything on the turn of that one all-important card.

Taking her hand in his, Joe asked quietly, "Mona Santiago, will you marry me?"

Her flight instincts fought for control of her. But as she began to pull her hand away, Joe tightened his grasp, holding her in place. Excitement and panic grabbed equal shares of her.

Was he really serious, or was this some elaborate joke on his part? "Why are you asking me that?" she asked breathlessly.

"Because I'm taking a survey," Joe snapped out in disgust. "Why do you think?" He was fairly shouting now and for once, he didn't care. His emotions were all spilling out. "Because I love you. And I'd rather spend the rest of my life fighting with you than having a peaceful relationship with anyone else." Still holding her hand tightly in his, he gave her a moment to absorb his words. "Now, what's your answer, Mona? Will you marry me?"

She struggled to fight back the panic. This was for forever and she knew it. "Don't rush me," she told him.

Was she serious? he thought incredulously. "I've been waiting for you all of my life, Mona. Even a snail wouldn't call this 'rushing.'"

She blew out a breath, then looked at her brother, who had been a silent witness to all this. Much as she loved him, she didn't want him here. This was just between her and Joe. For now.

"Do you mind?" she asked Rick.

His lips pulled back into a grin that threatened to split open his face. "Hell, no," Rick answered.

Did she have to explain everything? "I'm not asking your permission, I'm asking you to leave the office," Mona told him irritably.

"Silver tongued as always." Rick shifted around the side of his desk and crossed to the door. He glanced back at Joe for a split second. "I'd think about this long and hard if I were you, Joe. This is her good side."

"No, it's not," Joe murmured as Rick closed the door behind himself. "I've seen the good side," he continued, his eyes on Mona's, "and that's the side that'll keep me coming back for more."

The door was closed now. For all intents and purposes, they were alone, although he was aware that Alma, Larry and Rick were all outside, only a few feet away and only marginally pretending not to be looking into the inner office.

"I'm still waiting for an answer, Mona," he told her softly. Maybe this *was* too much pressure for her. He relented a little, not wanting to back her into a corner. "If you don't want to give me one now—"

She didn't wait for him to finish. "Don't tell me what I want or don't want, Joe."

Rather than comment on what she'd just said, he looked at her for a timeless moment. "I'm afraid, too, Mona."

Her back went up. To be afraid was to be vulnerable. She refused to appear to be vulnerable. People lost everything that way. The weak had their feelings trampled on. "I didn't say I was afraid."

"You didn't have to," he answered. He resisted taking

her into his arms. First, he was going to say his piece. "It's there, in your eyes. You're afraid that if you let your guard down, if you let yourself actually expect something, it's all going to blow up on you, leaving you with nothing."

She wanted to deny it, to tell him that he was letting his imagination run away with him. But there was no hiding from the truth.

"Maybe," Mona allowed with a careless shrug of her shoulder.

Unable to stand back any longer, Joe slipped his hands around her waist, holding her to him. He saw the battle to resist take place in her eyes. She remained where she was.

He was wearing her down, he thought in subdued triumph.

"I'm not going anywhere, Mona," he promised. "No matter how much you push me away, I'm not going anywhere."

"You just were," she pointed out.

His eyes smiled at her. His lips followed. "That was before I knew you loved me."

Her shoulders stiffened. "I didn't say that."

"Yeah, you did," he contradicted. "I'm as afraid as you are for the same reasons that you are," he assured her. "But if we love each other, then we can make this work."

Mona pressed her lips together. A single word escaped. "Yes." She made no effort to rein it in, to explain it away.

Joe was both surprised and pleased. "You're agreeing with me. This *is* a special day," he teased.

Ever contrary—it was a difficult habit to break—she shook her head. "No, I didn't say yes I agreed with you."

His head began to hurt. "Was there an instruction manual that came the day you were born?" he asked. "Because if there is one, I'll do anything to get my hands on it."

You'll have to be satisfied with getting your hands on me, she thought, suppressing a grin of her own.

"I said 'yes' to your marriage proposal," she told him. "And there's no manual," she went on to inform him. "You're just going to have to keep learning through hands-on experience."

Joe's face lit up like the sky on the Fourth of July. It made him look like the kid he'd been when he first saw her. "I can live with that."

"You'd better," she told him, threading her arms around his neck. "For a long, long time."

"I'll do my very best," Joe promised, lowering his mouth to hers.

And in so doing, he opened the door to their very own private paradise.

Neither one of them heard the three people outside the small office applauding, or Larry loudly declaring, "Finally." They heard nothing because they were lost in their own world and weren't about to try to find their way back anytime soon.

* * * * *

Don't miss the next book in
Marie Ferrarella's Forever, Texas series:
The Doctor's Forever Family.

COMING NEXT MONTH

Available February 8, 2011

HARCNM0111

REQUEST YOUR FREE BOOKS!
2 FREE NOVELS PLUS 2 FREE GIFTS!

Love, Home & Happiness!

YES! Please send me 2 FREE Harlequin® American Romance® novels and my 2 FREE gifts (gifts are worth about $10). After receiving them, if I don't wish to receive any more books, I can return the shipping statement marked "cancel." If I don't cancel, I will receive 4 brand-new novels every month and be billed just $4.24 per book in the U.S. or $4.99 per book in Canada. That's a saving of at least 15% off the cover price! It's quite a bargain! Shipping and handling is just 50¢ per book.* I understand that accepting the 2 free books and gifts places me under no obligation to buy anything. I can always return a shipment and cancel at any time. Even if I never buy another book from Harlequin, the two free books and gifts are mine to keep forever.

154/354 HDN E5LG

Name	(PLEASE PRINT)	
Address		Apt. #
City	State/Prov.	Zip/Postal Code

Signature (if under 18, a parent or guardian must sign)

Mail to the Harlequin Reader Service:
IN U.S.A.: P.O. Box 1867, Buffalo, NY 14240-1867
IN CANADA: P.O. Box 609, Fort Erie, Ontario L2A 5X3

Not valid for current subscribers to Harlequin® American Romance® books.

Want to try two free books from another line?
Call 1-800-873-8635 or visit www.morefreebooks.com.

* Terms and prices subject to change without notice. Prices do not include applicable taxes. N.Y. residents add applicable sales tax. Canadian residents will be charged applicable provincial taxes and GST. Offer not valid in Quebec. This offer is limited to one order per household. All orders subject to approval. Credit or debit balances in a customer's account(s) may be offset by any other outstanding balance owed by or to the customer. Please allow 4 to 6 weeks for delivery. Offer available while quantities last.

Your Privacy: Harlequin is committed to protecting your privacy. Our Privacy Policy is available online at www.eHarlequin.com or upon request from the Reader Service. From time to time we make our lists of customers available to reputable third parties who may have a product or service of interest to you. If you would prefer we not share your name and address, please check here. ☐

Help us get it right—We strive for accurate, respectful and relevant communications. To clarify or modify your communication preferences, visit us at www.ReaderService.com/consumerschoice.

HAR10R

HARLEQUIN®

A Romance

FOR EVERY MOOD™

Spotlight on
Classic

Quintessential, modern love stories
that are romance at its finest.

See the next page
to enjoy a sneak peek from
the Harlequin® Romance series.

*Harlequin Romance author Donna Alward is loved
for her gorgeous rancher heroes.*

*Meet Wyatt as he's confronted by both a precious
little pink bundle left on his doorstep and his neighbor Elli
who's going to show him the ropes....*

Introducing
PROUD RANCHER, PRECIOUS BUNDLE

THE SQUAWKING QUIETED as Elli picked the baby up, and
Wyatt turned around, trying hard to ignore the feelings of
inadequacy as Darcy immediately stopped fussing.

"Maybe she's uncomfortable. What do you think, sweet-
heart?" Elli turned her conversation to the baby.

"What do you think is wrong?" Wyatt asked, putting the
coffee pot back on the burner.

A strange look passed over Elli's face, one that looked
like guilt and panic. But it was gone quickly. "I couldn't
say," she replied.

"But you were so good with her this afternoon." Wyatt
put his hands on his hips.

"Lucky, that's all. I just...remembered a few things."
The same strange look flitted over her features once more.

Wyatt took the coffee to the table. "You fooled me. You
looked like you knew exactly what you were doing." So
much so that Wyatt had felt completely inept. A feeling he
despised. He was used to being the one in control.

Elli and Darcy walked the length of the kitchen and
back. After a few moments, she admitted, "I haven't really
cared for a baby before. The things I thought of were simply
things I'd heard about. Not from experience, Mr. Black."

Her chin jutted up, closing the subject but making him

want to ask the questions now pulsing through his mind. But then he remembered the old saying—*Don't look a gift horse in the mouth.* He'd benefit from whatever insight she had and be glad of it.

"I don't really know what babies need," he said. "I fed her, patted her back like you did, walked her to sleep, but every time I put her down…"

Wyatt almost groaned. Of course. He'd forgotten one important thing. He'd been so focused on getting the formula the right temperature that he'd forgotten to check her diaper. Not that he had any clue what to do there either.

Pulling calves and shoveling out stalls was far less intimidating than one tiny newborn.

"She's probably due for a diaper change, isn't she." He tried to sound nonchalant. This was a perfect opportunity. Elli must know how to change a diaper. He could simply watch her so he'd know better for the next time.

Instead, Elli came around the corner of the counter and placed Darcy back in his arms. "Here you go, Uncle Wyatt," she said lightly. "You get diaper duty. I'll fix the coffee. Cream and sugar?"

Oh boy, Wyatt thought, looking down into Darcy's pursed face, his smug plan blown to smithereens. He was in for it now.

Will sparks fly between Elli and Wyatt?

Find out in
PROUD RANCHER, PRECIOUS BUNDLE
Available February 2011 from Harlequin Romance

Try these Healthy and Delicious Spring Rolls!

INGREDIENTS

2 packages rice-paper spring roll wrappers (20 wrappers)

1 cup grated carrot

¼ cup bean sprouts

1 cucumber, julienned

1 red bell pepper, without stem and seeds, julienned

4 green onions finely chopped— use only the green part

DIRECTIONS

1. Soak one rice-paper wrapper in a large bowl of hot water until softened.

2. Place a pinch each of carrots, sprouts, cucumber, bell pepper and green onion on the wrapper toward the bottom third of the rice paper.

3. Fold ends in and roll tightly to enclose filling.

4. Repeat with remaining wrappers. Chill before serving.

Find this and many more delectable recipes including the perfect dipping sauce in

NTRSERIESJAN